MW00640352

MILWAUKEE DEEP

AN AMBROSE NOBEL NOVEL

 **SUBPLOT**

www.mascotbooks.com

Milwaukee Deep

©2023 Kirstie Croga. All Rights Reserved. No part of this publication may be reproduced, stored in a retrieval system or transmitted in any form by any means electronic, mechanical, or photocopying, recording or otherwise, without the permission of the author.

This is a work of fiction. Names, characters, businesses, places, events, and incidents are either the products of the author's imagination or used in a fictitious manner. Any resemblance to actual persons, living or dead, or actual events is purely coincidental.

For more information, please contact:
Subplot Publishing, an imprint of Amplify Publishing Group
620 Herndon Parkway, Suite 320
Herndon, VA 20170
info@mascotbooks.com

Library of Congress Control Number: 2022909254

CPSIA Code: PRV1122A

ISBN-13: 978-1-63755-559-0

Printed in the United States

To Philomena

AN AMBROSE NOBEL NOVEL

MILWAUKEE DEEP

KIRSTIE CROGA

SUBPLOT

A mass of gravity lies beneath the Puerto Rico Trench so dense it has a gravitational pull on the ocean, creating a visible dip on the surface and causing navigational instruments to malfunction. Eight hundred miles long, 60 miles wide, the trench encompasses the deepest point in the Atlantic Ocean, Milwaukee Deep. Milwaukee Deep, named for the American naval vessel that discovered it in 1939, plunges 5.2 miles from Earth's sheath. Earth smirks at Milwaukee Deep's name, knowing He has courted Her for millennia before humans even had language, fingering Her churning molten root, tickling tantric, inviting Her smoldering nectar to rise and fall in prolonged pleasure. In the universe's primordial foreplay, humans, their logic, and their language are insignificant. The solid ground they strive for, the love and land they die for, is just the veneered surface, dwarfed in the lusted coupling of gods tectonic. Eventually, She will peak.

CHAPTER 1

"You're wrong."

She stands, left foot pointing toward the back of the full room with the other steadying her from behind, the ingrained stance of a fighter to anyone well versed enough to recognize it. Waves of untamed auburn hair curtain her face before falling to her waist. Toast-masters would advise she corral her hair neatly into a tidy bun, creating a perception of openness and honesty with her audience, but doing so would be dishonest. She is not open. She does not connect easily.

She is striking, intriguing, strong. She turns pretty into potent. A hugging knee-length gray skirt and low-cut white blouse hint at generous curves. Teal glasses compete with pyre-blue eyes. She meant to wear her brown glasses today but couldn't find them.

"The well-meaning trauma-informed care model is the best we've got, and it's wrong. You've spent the semester learning about the model, and I appreciate your professor allowing me to offer a different perspective. So, tell me what'cha know." She could hear the scuffle of two hundred pairs of feet in the uncomfortable silence.

After a few minutes, a confident young woman with blond, news

-anchor-straight hair, wearing a smart, sensible suit, answers: "The trauma-informed care model is an approach that strives to create a safe space for victims of trauma and avoids retraumatizing them, especially among providers of services those victims will most likely encounter—doctors, teachers, human service organizations, the justice system, even libraries."

"Sounds great. How?"

"The first tenet is trustworthiness and transparency," she continues brightly. "Keep appointments; show up on time; make sure prescriptions are filled; be open and upfront about delays or problems." Her voice lowers sympathetically as she explains. "People who have experienced trauma have a difficult time trusting. You can build trust through small actions."

Her tone annoys Ambrose Nobel.

"That's nice. So, to help people recover from brutal, sustained traumas, we should use our words with care. Do what you say you are going to do; follow through; don't lie?"

"Simply put, yes," the student says with finality.

"That is great business advice. Great relationship advice. Great decent-human-being advice. But have truth and honesty become so rare it needs to be defined as part of someone else's recovery? If you're a liar, that's on you. If you don't show up, that's on you. If you can't keep your word, that's on you. That has *nothing* to do with someone else's trauma. I propose our society's rarity of truth and honesty sets the stage for continued tolerance of abuse."

"Maybe," says the news-desk-ready student, now committed to her public assertion. "But we can't fix everything. The trauma-informed care model is better than the alternative. A non-trauma-informed system punishes and blames your adult actions and asks, 'What is wrong with you?' A trauma-informed system holds you accountable for your actions but gives space to process what happened to you."

Ambrose knows on what page in which book the student, so ready for her close-up, has mined that catchy academic mantra she now clings to with the righteous certitude of fool's gold.

"And who holds the perpetrator of the trauma accountable?"

"That's a presumptuous question," the young woman counters. "You are assuming that all trauma stems from an individual that *can* be held accountable. Trauma can stem from poverty or neighborhood crime—those are pervasive community issues for which one person is not accountable."

"Quite right. I would further that by saying *all* trauma is a pervasive community issue. Even trauma perpetrated by a single individual relies on often subtle community condonement."

"But the model gives us a concrete, actionable, achievable pathway to help the victim find comfort and break the cycle of trauma. You are talking about much larger and more vague issues of challenging societal attitudes and values. What is your plan to address those?"

"I don't pretend to know. But I theorize the trauma-informed care model is addressing the wrong problem." Ambrose chooses this moment to relax her stance, taking in the earnest, engaged faces lining the staggered rows of the amphitheater before continuing. *She's just a kid*, Ambrose thinks to herself. *Her heart is in the right place. Her tenacity will serve her well.* Ambrose remembers her objective, which is not to be drawn into contention but to draw others toward understanding.

"My goal is to bridge the divide that separates those who have and those who have not experienced trauma. It's a divide I have come to think about as a hidden element of diversity. We know the solution to embracing diversity is altering community attitudes to celebrate the strengths of other cultures—their foods, their music, their arts, their style. That kind of community change *is* achievable. I suggest we do the same: embrace the inherent strengths of a survivor's mindset instead of trying to fix it."

"But that survivor mindset is dangerous." Not a strand of hair moves out of place as she shakes her head, disagreeing. "Trauma lashes out, creates antisocial behaviors, and perpetuates continued suffering. A survivor's brain is wired to overreact to saber-toothed tigers that no longer exist."

"Do they not?" asked Ambrose, one eyebrow raised.

The perky young woman pauses a moment, traces of exasperation in her cover-girl face.

"This model has been based on research by some of the foremost PhDs in the field. I have missed your qualifications," she challenges.

"My qualifications? I have no PhD. I'm not a doctor or a psychologist. Your prof is rather liberal to allow me to speak to you, as I do so solely because I am passionate about advocating for a different conversation. I am not qualified to teach this class. Hell, I may not even be qualified to take this class."

The news-anchor wannabe grows smug.

"But I did start fighting saber-toothed tigers when I was about seven, and I assure you they still exist. I was the little girl threatened with having her skull bashed in. I was the little girl watching clouds go by, trying to forget the reek of seafood on his breath. And I am the woman she grew up to be—the client who will walk into your clinic."

She allows an uncomfortable silence to settle. The deliberate hiatus is meant to be uncomfortable. One of Ambrose's greatest strengths is being comfortable being uncomfortable.

"My teachers didn't protect me. My family didn't protect me. My doctors didn't protect me. My church didn't protect me. What protection I had, I gave myself. The abuse didn't stop because I learned to breathe deeply or rub lavender oil on my third eye or use 'I feel' words. It stopped because I grew strong and cunning. It stopped because I learned when to hide and when to fight. It stopped because of me."

The discomfort in the room now has gravity, weighing down even the smug young woman. Now they are listening.

"The trauma-informed care model naively invites the survivor to abandon whatever behavior or mechanism that allowed them to survive, to better blend into this ivory-tower world built upon the assumption that saber-toothed tigers are extinct. And because that world is built on that assumption, this approach does nothing to protect them. That is insane. It's insane to invite a survivor to be an accomplice to the very system that allowed their trauma to occur in the first place.

"This condescending model tries to fix survivors as if they are the broken ones. I am not broken. A society that leaves children to defend themselves against saber-toothed tigers they won't admit exist, and then wants to correct them for understandable behaviors they adopt to fight them off . . . that . . . is broken."

———————

She stands at the doorway speaking with a few stragglers eager to share their own experiences. The irony is, she hates this part. She speaks out so that others can find their voice, to improve communication between those who have and those who have not had traumatic pasts, to change thinking, to have exactly *this* conversation. But she is emotionally exhausted. Assuredness, or maybe arrogance, makes public speaking easy for her, but the vulnerability of laying herself bare before strangers drains her.

A slight ring emits from her phone. Her heart quickens in a purely Pavlovian response, her chest now crimson against her white, low-cut blouse.

Glancing down at her Android, she slides the Snap. A blurred picture reveals a gruff Irish face, unkempt curls, a scruffy beard and shows bare, imposing shoulders, inked with Celtic tribal runes.

im gonna choke you

Her eyes flicker as she reaches for her water bottle before purposefully turning her attention back to the last of the students who have summoned the courage to approach her.

CHAPTER 2

H er white cami is drenched with sweat, revealing a pink sports bra. Her waist-long hair has been casually braided and swings to the side below pink headsets, whose pounding beat drowns out the raw, clanking rhythms of the fight club.

Her curvaceous frame formerly outlined by the gray skirt and white blouse is now on full display. At five feet eight inches tall, she is a strong, full-figured woman. Her build lends itself to boxing and kickboxing, which come naturally, given her muscular legs and defined shoulders, affording enough extra weight to throw into a punch.

Alone in thought, she is intense, focused. She executes her signature series: jab, cross, jab, push kick landing into southpaw, uppercut, hook, elbow, spinning backhand. Again. And again. It looks all brutal fury. It is not. Her moves are controlled. The motions purposeful. The combination has taken years to master. It will take many more years to perfect. She repeats, keeping cadence with the music in her headsets, not the trash metal one might expect but the smooth sensual vocals of Annie Lennox:

I put a spell on you 'cause you're mine.

Again. And again. Each strike, each step is lovingly executed. Stopping. Thinking. Slowing. Again. Focus.

She startles when she feels a hand on her shoulder and pivots, instinctively stance ready with gloves caging her jaws.

"Don't hit me," a smirked mouth buried in a blondish beard that matches tousled curls speaks, "and for Christ's sake don't elbow me." Her heart quickens, once more Pavlovian at the sight of his endearingly quirky smile.

"Gonna let me choke ya?"

Her gloves lower, revealing a cocky grin. She rips the Velcro from her gloves with her teeth, shakes them to the floor, and beckons him forward, black wraps still steadying her wrists and hands.

They circle a few moments before she shoots angled, grabbing his wrist and wrapping his leg in an attempted fireman's carry. She overshoots and fails to secure his arm. He is quick to seize the advantage. He takes her into a guillotine on the way to the mat. She manages to create space and shrimp out of his grip. They roll, snaked, matted, and withered. She frames, centers, bridges him over her. She works to cradle his head between her thighs, trying to grasp his throat in the bended crux of her knee, but she doesn't secure a tight lock, leaving him room.

He exploits the advantage again, releasing from her legs while still holding them, ensnaring her quickly, his legs wrapping her hips from behind. He hauls her back, forcing a rear naked chokehold, thick arms boaing her neck, strong legs hooking hers.

"Tap," he says.

"No."

His legs pull her closer, tightening her against his body, arching her back to a tight stretch, limiting her ability to move. Though tall and thick herself, his six-foot-three-inch broad frame engulfs her.

"Tap, darlin'," he whispers in her ear.

"No!"

His bicep forms a noose around her neck, slowly strangling her.

"Taaaap," he insists.

She struggles against him once more, rolls her eyes, lets out an exasperated "uggggg," and taps. She never wins. He immediately releases her and jumps up, offering his hand. Reluctantly she takes it, slow to get up. She refuses to grow accustomed to losing.

"You're vicious on your feet. But most fights don't end on your feet. You need a better ground game."

"I know," she sulks.

"You're too aggressive."

"Too aggressive? It's a fucking fight!"

"No, Ambrose. It's a sport. You practice the sport so you can be calm and logical in a fight. You panic; you overreact; you waste energy. You're forcing it. You're trying to use your strength instead of your leverage. Ya gotta learn to breathe into it, literally roll with your momentum and use theirs against them. Don't give up your back. Protect your neck. Keep your frame. Stay on your opponent's center line. And keep calm through the panic. Breathe into it," he lectures passionately.

She looks up at him moodily, giving him a grudging nod.

He softens at the earnestness in her large blue eyes, which he knows are stunningly beautiful and stunningly beautiful only. He knows they function poorly as a means of sight. He also knows her to be an eager, invested student with a natural aggressiveness and tenacity he can't train. But she is emotionally delicate and guarded, slow to warm and quick to cool.

"You have to time that fireman's carry better. It should be one fluid motion. You have the technique down. Now you need the art of timing it so you use your opponent's momentum against them."

They go through the motions of timing the fireman's carry a few times until she becomes frustrated.

"Enough for today. Ya know I choke you outta love, right?" he says, smiling.

She tilts her head the way curious, lop-eared puppies do and reaches out to him, fingertips brushing his rash guard just below his navel. "I know."

Her touch lingers, feeling his veeing abs through his rash guard.

Their eyes linger too. The intensity of the fight has not yet left them.

"Hey, Ambrose, when are you are going to roll with the rest of us?" calls a boy whose match has ended on the adjacent mat.

"You know she only rolls with Marcus," says another.

"She's too high-class. All intellectual and shit. The chick hangs out at the fucking library," another roller teases. Ambrose responds with an eye roll.

"She does hang out in the library. You goons could uplift your sorry-assed selves by hanging out in the library once in a while. She would embarrass you on the mat anyway," Marcus defends. "Reset the timer and let's roll."

Grateful Marcus has provided a distraction, she tosses her discarded gloves into a worn bag, throws on a weathered gray Title sweatshirt, and heads toward the door. Glancing back, she searches for Marcus instinctively before leaving and finds him doing the same. He smiles, showing that fighter's grin, and grasps his neck with his hands in a teasing choking motion.

Smirking sarcastically toward him, she cusses under her breath.

CHAPTER 3

Throwing her glove bag and sweatshirt in the disorderly entryway of her small Philadelphia apartment, she struggles to pull off the cami plastered to her body with sweat. Passing a full-length mirror, she stops, poses, and takes in her body. She twists at the waist, smiling at the sight of long, shapely legs sweeping upward toward a firm, peached ass. She shakes her hair loose from her warrior braid and lets the tresses fall to her waist, unkempt and still damp with sweat. She moves her head side to side, feeling the waves caress her back, and smiles, finding the comfort of her own hair as reassuring as a child's blanket, a hugging veil against the world.

Twisting back, her smile turns to a scowl as she glimpses the love handles and stubborn belly pooch she works so hard to eliminate, never quite succeeding. She discovers a large fresh bruise forming on her elbow. She touches it, winces, gives a last scowl, and tosses her cami into the washer. Cradling the tender bruise, she gingerly slips off her shorts and pulls on an oversize tee and pair of boy's boxers from the dryer. She grabs a water from the fridge, steps over a pile of books, and settles into a worn, comfortable couch with her laptop and a manila envelope just as her phone rings.

Glancing down at the name on the screen, she holds the phone for a moment.

"Shit," she mutters, as she hits the talk button.

"I'm on it, Will."

"Yeah?" His voice is soft, charming, affable.

"Yeah." She puts him on speaker and searches for a file on her laptop, hoping he can't hear the urgent tapping of the keys that testifies to how utterly unprepared she is for this call.

"'Cause I'm wondering if the fairest girl in Philly was hitting people instead of working on the Cortez manuscript I'm paying her to write." He is not angry. He is never angry. He is always patient. He is always "nice." It is a trait that endears him to those blind enough to buy into it and annoying to those who have learned how shallow he is. She is one who has learned. And she hates "nice." She hates him.

"You know I write better postfight," she deflects.

"I do not know that. I have never known you to be anything other than postfight. Except when you are midfight and mad at me."

She ignores the dig. He has never once seen her fight. His arrogance allows him to believe he has felt the full weight of her anger, her passion, when he's never come close to experiencing her brand of rage. She refuses to put her energy into challenging that arrogant assumption.

He pauses long enough to accept that his jab has failed to land.

"Are you looking for your glasses?" he chimes, changing tactics.

"No," she lies, snaking her hand between the cushions, fishing for the knockoff designer spectacles she orders online two pairs at a time.

"Need I remind you Rick Cortez's Aunt Philomena is dying? He wants to gift her at least the rough draft before she goes to her great reward. We gotta give that to him. Come on, fairest. You can write this in your sleep."

She snags her glasses from between the couch pillows and perches them on her nose, balancing her laptop and the manila envelope.

"Did you find them?"

"Yeah."

"So, where are you, fairest?" he taunts.

"Stop."

"OK," he concedes, and his voice straightens. "Where are you?"

"It will be done. I talked to Rick yesterday, and I'm meeting Aunt Philomena in person. First chapter is finished . . . I just . . ." She hesitates. She does not trust him. For good reason, and not even for the little things. But he is her publisher and editor. Ghostwriting for Hodges Inc. affords her a full-time salary with benefits, remote work, and a life of comfort and autonomy, with enough free time to train and write for herself. "It's just . . . I came across something kinda odd while researching the family in Puerto Rico."

"Yeah?" His voice conveys only passing interest.

"Yeah. OK. Stick with me for a minute on this . . ." Earnest intrigue overcomes her caution.

"I will always stick with you, if you allow me."

She ignores the suggestive implication, having learned long ago that he is all meaningless innuendo. He is a master of deception, of lingering words, cliffing phrases, reaping the benefit of others' jumps, allowing them to crash while he retains all innocence. Cruel kindness and false humility are his trademarks. He is a snake oil peddler. Gentle, pretty lies are his hallmark.

She loathes those so willing to buy his success at the price of their own dignity. She doesn't know why she hates them so much. But she does.

"Philomena's mother died of tuberculosis when Philomena was a child. And at first glance, that fits. They were living in the slums of a Puerto Rican island in the early 1940s, dirt poor, in crowded conditions, probably malnourished with inadequate medical care . . . " She lingers there.

"OK. Then what's the issue?"

"Eleven children were living in that shanty, plus the grandfather and other relatives, all malnourished, all lacking medical care. All eleven kids, save for those killed in World War II, grow up healthy and are still alive to this day."

"And thank goodness for that so our client can pay us to write the family story," quips Will.

"Why did they survive, Will? How does one person slowly die of a highly contagious disease in a cramped shanty shared with fifteen other people and *not one of them* ever gets sick? It doesn't make sense."

This time he pauses with genuine thoughtfulness. Sincerity is a rare quality in him.

"Good point. Maybe a resistant family gene? Same as the plague. By definition those who survived were immune and passed on the immunity?" His interest is piqued, his long-dead reporter instincts prickling.

"Right, but the Cortezes aren't the only ones. I did some research and dug through genealogy records. The Cortez case is not an anomaly. During the 1940s, on the island of Vieques, an inordinate number of death certificates list the cause of death as tuberculosis, but the epidemiology doesn't fit."

"Maybe those doctors weren't familiar enough with the disease to make accurate diagnoses?"

"Is diagnoses really the plural of diagnosis?"

"Yep." She could hear the smugness in his voice. He knew she was fascinated by words. For all his faults, and he was mostly faults, he was a very, very good editor.

"Either way," she said dismissively, refusing to admire him even for what was admirable, "Puerto Rico was scathingly familiar with the disease."

"Scathingly?" he toys.

"Scathingly," she repeats. "The island had a history of persistent breakouts, enough so that there were TB sanitoriums on mainland Puerto Rico. But in the 1940s, a huge increase in cases was reported on Vieques, and many of those cases don't fit the spread pattern of TB."

"A case of overworked caregivers who didn't have time to properly diagnose or treat?"

"Maybe. Maybe they were overwhelmed and just attributed anything with coughing to TB. But that still doesn't answer the question: If it wasn't TB, what was it? What was the proper diagnosis? Or diagnoses? Wait, if more than one person receives the identical diagnosis, is it a diagnosis or diagnoses? Is the plural attributed to the number of people or the number of diseases?"

"That is a discussion best had over drinks. The TB disparity is intriguing," he concedes. "Less intriguing but perhaps more urgent . . . when will the Cortez manuscript be done?"

"I'm on it. I am starting right now, even before we hang up." She mashes a smattering of keys on the keyboard for effect.

"Yes, I hear your overly obvious typing. Thank you, fairest. I know you won't let me down. You never have," he croons, the snake oil dripping from every syllable.

"Don't thank me. It's not about you. I won't let Rick and Philomena down," she corrects him. She's careful to never miss a chance to remind him that dedication to her work is never, *ever* about him.

"So you will begin as soon as we hang up?"

"Hard to write while you're talking to me . . ."

"OK. Bye."

"Bye," she echoes with a tinge of sarcasm before punching the red phone icon.

She hesitates a moment.

"Fuck it," she mutters, glancing between the phone and her laptop before dialing a familiar number.

"Hey, got time for lunch? I have a pressing need to draw upon the expertise of my favorite cousin–slash–infectious disease doctor . . ."

CHAPTER 4

"**M**ycobacterium tuberculosis. You have to understand they are older than humans," he says.

"'They'?" she balks, her mouth half full of black bean salad. "You mean 'it.'"

"No, I mean 'they.'"

They are sitting in a hospital cafeteria, her red tray kitty-cornered to make way for her notebook while his tray is perfectly aligned with the edge of the Formica table. His name tag reads "Kevin Cooper, MD, DrPH."

He pulls the bread from his sandwich gingerly with his thumb and pointer finger, removes three pickles, and places them neatly on an awaiting napkin. He makes a small origami-like package, which he places in a bowl sitting precisely at the top right of the tray. With a second napkin, he wipes his thumb and pointer finger clean and also places the napkin in the bowl.

She watches his ritual and smiles to herself. "Why did you ask f pickles if you don't want pickles?"

"I don't want pickles. I want the impression of pickles."

She pauses. Fighting has taught her valuable lessons a⊦ where to expend energy. She lets the pickled impressi

"Fine. What'da ya mean, 'they'?"

"'It' refers to a singular object. 'They' is the nominative plural of 'it.' Or so I believe. You're the writer."

"The writer I am. Technically, 'it' can also be used to represent a group—e.g., 'The group of people next to us wondered why someone would order a pickled sandwich and then take off the pickles'—and 'they' can be used to represent a singular collective—e.g., 'The pickles were taken from the sandwich on which they were just placed.' English is weird. And let's not forget King's *It*."

"No one can forget King's *It*." He shudders. "I'll leave you to sort out the English, but I can assure you as an infectious disease specialist and medical epidemiologist that mycobacterium tuberculosis involves singular living beings residing in colonies."

"TB is alive?" She makes a freak-show face.

"Of course. Bacteria are like all living beings. They have an imperative to survive, to procreate, to thrive. TB is one of the most successful beings on the planet."

"You sound as though you admire them. These microscopic creepies make people sick. They kill people, Kev."

"I do admire them. Host illness ensures their survival. You're judging them based on your own species's desire for survival, which is also natural. But, objectively, humans have expended a great deal of resources eradicating TB. And they have failed. TB precedes humans by billions of years and, were I to guess, will supersede humans by billions of years. If we don't destroy the planet first."

"Well, humans do waste a good deal of pickles," she mutters before growing serious. "Tell me this. Do any other diseases mimic TB closely enough to be misdiagnosed?"

"Of course. A subject can be infected with TB and remain asymptomatic in what is referred to as latent TB. The bacteria remain dormant during a host's period of good health when the immune system prevents the bacteria om multiplying. The carrier is not sick and not contagious. All's well until the immune system is stressed, malnourished, or fighting another infection or disease, at which point the bacteria become active and multiply."

"Exploiting their prey's weakness. I have an editor with that trait."

"Yes, these are opportunistic organisms. The carrier becomes ill with active tuberculosis when the host becomes vulnerable. So there may not be an immediate connection between contracting the illness and displaying symptoms. In modern America, TB might be misdiagnosed as flu, pneumonia, or bronchitis."

"Aren't there tests in modern-day America?"

"Yes. People are regularly tested, especially before working in high-risk jobs."

"Like yours?"

"Like mine. Medical staff. Prison guards. Childcare workers. But because the disease is rare in America and the symptoms mimic other far more common diseases, it is possible that a case of TB could go undetected for some time."

"What about in 1940s Puerto Rico?"

"Nineteen-forties Puerto Rico?"

"Nineteen-forties Puerto Rico," she reiterates.

"I haven't reviewed specific data sets for that population, but if you are asking, generally, conditions supporting tuberculosis outbreaks would be in place in 1940s Puerto Rico—poverty, poor medical care, civil unrest, the beginning of mass travel, war . . ."

"War. That's right. Nineteen forties . . . Second World War."

"War brings mass human migration, interaction between soldiers and indigenous populations, weapons, waves of refugees, starvation, stress, factors that can affect health outcomes for generations. Disease has played a role in every war since the beginning of war. During the Bl? Death, plague-ridden bodies would be catapulted into sieged ? The Vietcong enticed American soldiers with prostitutes inf? STDs. Dysentery alone has had a far greater effect on so? humanly constructed military advancement."

"I hadn't thought about the war," she says, processing the deluge of information.

"Then you have an incomplete picture."

"Riddle me this. A fifteen-person poverty-stricken family living in a shanty during the 1940s on a Puerto Rican island—Vieques. One of them dies of TB."

"Makes sense."

"But not one other family member dies. Not one of them *ever* gets sick with TB, not even to this day."

"That would give me pause, but anomalies happen."

"Is it possible for that anomaly to affect hundreds of families on one small island?"

"Not likely. That is incompatible with the epidemiology of tuberculosis."

Ambrose reaches into her backpack, offering him a worn manila envelope with crumpled edges. He looks with revulsion at the dirty, ragged package. She ignores his reaction.

"Look over these death certificates. Please? Something is very, very wrong," she implores him, suddenly serious. He acquiesces, taking the proffered envelope distastefully between his forefinger and thumb.

"Thank you," she says in earnest. Then, rising from the table to leave, she brightens. "Why would a germophobe become an infectious disease doctor? It's like a vegetarian working in a slaughterhouse."

"Because in the end, germs always win. I'm a sucker for lost causes. I've been to your apartment. You could do with a healthy dose of germaphobia."

"One more thing," she says, turning back with a smile, remembering fondly their childhood mantra designed to extend their goodbyes. "One more thing: plural of 'diagnosis'?"

"'Diagnoses.'"

"Several diagnoses of one person or several people with the same ¡agnosis?"

He thinks, perplexed. "I hadn't ever thought about that."

"Maybe now's a good time."

"One more thing," he calls after her. "There's a family reunion coming up . . ."

Her smile fades, and the remembered fondness of their childhood turns dark and walled. He sees her energy shift, her eyes wander. He pushes just a bit more.

"Ambrose, your parents didn't do anything."

She inhales, unconsciously rising to a fighting stance, aims a seething gaze at him more powerful than she is aware of, and exhales. "Exactly."

Then she is gone.

Kev sighs and gathers himself. She is all kinetic energy that is both captivating and draining. He is accustomed to the need to decompress after seeing her. He slowly shakes his head and mutters to himself, "Love ya, cuz. We all do."

CHAPTER 5

Her royal-blue Dodge Dart slowly pulls into the parking lot. It is dark, after nine o'clock. She strains her neck, hoping for a beacon of light from inside the Ground Zero Fight Club.

She has no idea what Marcus does outside of Ground Zero. She doesn't know where he lives, if he owns a business besides Ground Zero, what he eats, if he enjoys a good bourbon, if he goes to church, if he has a girlfriend.

But she does know he keeps a collection of war memorabilia, has an encyclopedic knowledge of battle strategy, and liberally cites *The Art of War* and Jefferson's famed quote about watering the tree of liberty. She teased him once, asking if he be patriot or tyrant. He countered by asking why she assumed the two were mutually exclusive.

He has told her many times to stop by anytime, whether the club is open or not. She sees a weak stream of light and parks the car, thinking now *is* anytime.

Jumping over the curb, she tests the club's door. It opens. A ribbon of light peeks from behind a closed rec room adjacent to Marcus' at the back of the club. She lunges across the gym, avoiding pads and shields in the dark, enters his dim office, and no weapons and battle maps mounted on the wall. Voices, laughter, and the swishing of an opened can filters toward her from the rec room door. She stops, suddenly feeling like an intruder, a stalker. She closes her eyes in embarrassment and turns to leave just as the peeking light widens and the rec door opens.

Wincing, she slowly turns to face her humiliation. He stands, an imposing figure in the doorway, until he laughs in surprised recognition. "Ambrose?"

"Hi." Her voice is tin and weak. She is mortified. How had she thought this surprise visit was a good idea? It was bad enough for him to know she had come in the first place but worse for him to catch her sneaking out. He towers in the doorway, bemused, almost triumphant. A man driven by the fight, he is intoxicated by the high ground ceded him by so careful an opponent.

"Come to train?" he teases. "Privates are expensive."

The mix of sounds streaming from the adjacent room suddenly becomes louder. Slurred voices. Girls' slurred voices. The sharp smell of liquor and clouds of dank muskiness roll into the room. He may be intoxicated by more than having won the high ground. She begins to comprehend the enormity of her overstep, and somehow it strengthens her. "I'm sorry . . . I shouldn't be here."

He glances back to the room, closes the door, and feels his high ground slipping. "Nope, I told ya anytime. I meant it. I just . . . uhh . . . have some people over."

He hits the lights, jolting her with the sudden brightness.

"You're not obligated to explain to me. I shouldn't have come. I just stopped by to talk about . . . your guns," she says, realizing how hollow a pretext that sounds.

"You stopped by at nine at night to talk about my guns?" he repeats. "Woulda hoped for a better reason."

She feels the blood rushing to her cheeks, blushing uncharacteristically. Then she blushes because she blushes.

"But OK, if you want to talk about my guns at nine at night, let's do that." He wobbles a little, possibly annoyed and clearly intoxicated.

"You've been drinking."

"Honey, I've been doing a little more than that."

She shifts unconsciously to a more guarded stance.

"So . . . maybe more about war history than guns. World War II. Puerto Rico. What'da ya know? When I think of World War II, I don't think of Puerto Rico."

"That's incredibly random. But yeah, the US built huge naval bases in Puerto Rico during the war. Tactical importance. We lost more ships in the Caribbean than anywhere else in the world."

"Really? How?"

"German U-boats picking off every ship—military, civilian, commercial—cutting off supply chains. At one time Puerto Rico had the largest military base in the world. For good reason. If one of those islands fell to the Axis, we coulda been having this incredibly random conversation about my guns in German."

"What happened to the people who lived there?"

"Don't know. Relocated? Drafted? Married soldiers? I am sure many were not happy."

"Because the navy took their land?"

"They didn't just take the land. They destroyed it. Used it as proving grounds."

"Proving grounds for what?"

"Don't know. Target practice? Biological weapons? Maybe nukes? Whatever they did, the soil is still contaminated." He moves, a bit unsteady, toward her. "Behind you there's a . . ."

His sudden movement startles her. She flinches, instinctively raising her hands to protect her face.

He halts, startled himself by her reaction. He cautiously raises a hand, open palmed, then slowly points behind her, directing her gaze to a World War II–era map on his wall. Realizing yet another blunder, she blushes again.

She is saved from having to respond by a cute blonde stumbling in from the rec room. Perfect and frilly and girly, the blonde's lacy half shirt shows model-flat abs, with none of Ambrose's stubborn love handles. She has artfully highlighted hair, perfectly contoured makeup, and long, lacquered nails. Ambrose unconsciously clenches her own nubby fingernails, always short and stained from leathered gloves. The perfect blonde stumbles into Marcus's arms, purposely wedging herself between them. "Markie, where have you been? Come back to the party. I miiiiiiss you," she slurs.

"Markie?" Ambrose mouths to him, raising an eyebrow. "Do you have a boy band now?"

The blonde turns to Ambrose as though she has just noticed her. "Hiiiii. I'm Tiffani. With an 'i'."

"Of course you are," says Ambrose, not hiding the sarcasm in her voice.

"What are you two doing in here? Are you holding out on us? Do you have some good shit or something?" the blonde whines in a high voice.

"No, I don't have any shit," Ambrose says disdainfully. "I was just leaving."

"She trains here," Marcus explains to the blonde.

"OMG. You fight? Oh, is that like your schtick? I guess some girls have to have a schtick," she croons in a condescending, drunken-valley-girl way. "Should I be afraid? Are you going to like punch me or something? Markie, you'll protect me, right?"

"Get her away from me . . . Markie," Ambrose mimics over the blonde's head. Marcus nods, already guiding the Barbie doll back to the party as Ambrose quickly makes her way out of the gym. This time she doesn't look back. She sits in her car, head resting on the steering wheel for a moment, processing how very, very wrong that went.

CHAPTER 6

Crisscross applesauce on her couch, nestled in a pillow fort of dog-eared books, safely tucked away from Marcus and blondes named Tiffani with an "i," she opens a notebook and attempts to untangle the timeline that is the US military's presence in Vieques.

While adept at online research and awed by the impeccable logic of databases, Ambrose still favors old textbooks for historical research, which lend insight into the events themselves and provide context about the time in which the books were written. She is fascinated by the drastically different interpretations of the same historic events taught to schoolchildren as official versions just a few years apart, showing how easily prevailing thought, cultural norms, and political tides reinterpret reality. Discrepancies are most noticeable in the decades immediately following the event, before the story settles into history.

To Ambrose, history isn't static but characterized by shifting, dynamic movements that influence across time. History is found in the interplay—the study of the animated contra dance between past, present, and future, where leads shift with tempo. Nowhere, at least nowhere accessible from her comfy couch, are those shifts more apparent than in the written words a society has committed to teaching its children.

This time, her method has failed. Studying the history of Vieques through textbooks proves difficult. She finds little mention of the island at all, as if Vieques, a fifty-two-square-mile island inhabited by ten thousand souls, simply doesn't exist, except as a dot on a map, robbed of even the dignity of a label.

She considers the lack of acknowledgment of Vieques as context itself. She is forced to rely on a handful of well-written books, scant academic papers, a few organizations dedicated to cultural preservation, suspect government dossiers, and, God forbid, Wikipedia to begin to disentangle and piece together the island's history.

VIEQUES

Born in the wrestling of tectonic plates, the Caribbean plate clutching east while the North American plate grappled west, the earth's core labored for millennia before Vieques crested its ocean womb 190 million years ago. Birthed in strife, it was abandoned to relentless assault from two oceans, the Atlantic to its north, the Caribbean to its south. Its youth was troubled, exploding continuously from its birth in the Jurassic period through the Tertiary period 2.6 million years ago, before it calmed. Its temper softened, the cinders from its youthful wrath giving way to rich, fertile soil and a plethora of natural anomalies whose presence together on one tiny island is mythical, perhaps even mystical.

Memories of its angry youth nurtures Monte Pirata, the island's highest peak, which feeds the beach cradled at its base of volcanic bedrock, creating extremely fine, heavy sand that is coal black and magnetic. To the west, a nursery of red mangroves, warm water, and small ocean channels foster a bay rich in single-celled bioluminescent dinoflagellates, creating the most intense glowing cove in the world. Vieques's volcanic peaks bookend the island, connected by a central ridge and valleyed with a lush lowland sloping to tropical beaches. Sharp nearshore islets break the unending ocean horizon.

The island lacks a natural fresh running water source, with no permanent lakes or streams, but is dotted with sapphire lagoons, mangrove swamps, salt flats, and coral reefs. The fruits of Vieques are the tangy flesh of mango, nutrient-dense sweet potatoes, versatile plantains, rich avocados, earthen coconut, and an endless supply of seafood.

Lying just west of Puerto Rico and east of the Virgin Islands, Vieques measures just 20 miles from east to west, 4.5 miles wide. The paradise island is just one of many freckling the silhouette between the Atlantic Ocean and the Caribbean, close enough for early seafarers to reach.

It came to know man three thousand years B.C., when Indigenous hunter-gatherers traversed the island. Some of the oldest human remains in the Caribbean are found in Vieques, as well as mysterious purposeful rock formations that whisper the ancient's universal knowing and elaborate rituals.

Over centuries, waves of mariners from Venezuela and Cuba, along with island-hopping Arawak Indians, navigated to the island and mingled with the natives, forming the gentle Taino culture. Highly organized into kingdoms with demigods who controlled the universe and communed through medicine men, the Taino, whose name translates to "good and noble," were a happy, friendly people, resting on hammocks and banana leaf beds, fishing and farming and dancing and drinking wine. They lived in peace, save for occasional raids from their cannibalistic Carib neighbors.

Columbus's arrival in the Caribbean may have constituted a discovery for Europeans, but the island had long been inhabited and cultivated by highly sophisticated peoples. Vieques, along with Puerto Rico, was claimed for the Spanish crown, an act that confused the natives who were unaware that land could be owned. The Taino of Vieques, true to their nature, welcomed the Spaniards in peace and shared the secrets of the island—how to make wine, repair boats and nets, and best enjoy the rich fruits of the island.

Having claimed the island and sapped the knowledge from the natives, the conquistadores set out to tame and control both. Seeing the devil's hand in the glowing bay, they dropped large boulders in the narrow channel to the ocean, lest the unholy waters be unleashed on the world. The Spaniards demanded impossible tariffs, effectively enslaving the natives. Many Taino, still not comprehending the idea of owning land, much less people, fled the island to escape oppression. Driven to warfare, they banded with their Carib enemies to mount attacks against the Spaniards. The attacks failed, and the Spanish retaliated with a ferocious genocide, slaughtering women and children alongside warriors, decimating the Taino, rendering the culture all but extinct. The genocide had no reason, no strategy, no logic. After brutally slaying an entire people, Spain simply abandoned the island.

Vieques grew restless and wild from neglect, the land itself absorbing the trauma of the Taino. Its intercourse with man, once gently seductive and enchanting, turned violent and abusive. While Spain maintained its claim to the island, it failed to defend or colonize it, leaving the fair isle open to constant attacks from the French, English, Dutch, Danes, and Prussians, who found Vieques equally easy to claim and impossible to secure.

The island proved best suited for those whose rules were more colloquial and decentralized. Like a defiant adolescent, Vieques embraced the era's raffish bad boys—lawless pirates. The romance betwixt island and pirate allowed both to buck paternal global tyranny in favor of independent localized anarchy.

As if on cue, a chirp from her phone announced the arrival of a Snap from 2nddegreemarcus.

talk?

Raffish bad boy, indeed, she thinks. Then aloud, she says, "No, Marcus, I do not desire a grown man acting like teenage boy bucking authority. I desire the authority."

With that declaration, she returns to the enchanting tale of Vieques without answering.

As dependence on ocean transport grew and shifting world politics brought its geography as a passage island into focus, Spain's fleeting attention once again returned to assert dominance on Vieques. The early nineteenth century brought its first governor, appointed by Spain and tasked with imposing order and making profitable the troublesome and untamed province. Seemingly cycling its history of trauma, the island was drawn and quartered into large parcels of land, sold to foreign interests, its verdant jungles burned and stripped to make way for sugarcane fields. Blood brothers of the land, an influx of slaves and migrant workers shared this brutal fate, mostly Blacks from neighboring islands. The slaves and near slaves brought with them distinct food and culture, and an ancient mysticism that congressed with stoic Spanish Catholicism to birth a unique spirituality, heady with a mix of communion and conjure, rosaries and roots, santos and gods.

The island's rich soil bore forced sugarcane as its own, nurturing the crop with ease and to plenty and, in doing so, ensuring its own continued exploitation. Foreign landowners grew in wealth on the sweat of slaves and the hard-won, ash-rich earth.

While global demand for sugar drove its economy, daily life on Vieques was isolated, and it was little felt when the island was ceded to the United States as part of the Treaty of Paris almost as an afterthought.

The early twentieth century brought economic pressures that decimated the sugarcane industry upon which the island was built. Many plantation owners simply abandoned their fields, the island, and the people. While legal slavery had been banished, the few remaining plantation owners formed a slavery of economics, paying appallingly low wages to workers who did backbreaking and often dangerous work: hoeing and planting, watering and threshing, boiling and pressing. The natives combined their meager plantation earnings with the gifts of the island—fishing and harvesting and sustenance farming land they didn't own—and found a proud, peaceful life. Under their hard work and resourcefulness, the island eased into its natural warmth, once more becoming friendly and hospitable. These Jibaro, as they came to call themselves, were proud of and deeply grateful for their simple, honest, and uncomplicated lives.

In 1917, President Wilson signed the Jones-Shafroth Act, granting statutory American citizenship to Puerto Ricans nineteen years after the island came into its possession. Statutory citizenship was limited, unprotected by the Constitution, and excluded both representation in Congress and the right to vote—conditions that exist to this day. Statutory citizenship, however, did make Puerto Ricans eligible for the compulsory draft that followed several months later upon the United States' entrance into World War I. Twenty thousand Puerto Rican men were drafted within weeks of gaining citizenship.

Ambrose stops a moment—it can't be right that Puerto Ricans still can't vote. A quick fact check reveals its truth: Puerto Ricans do not have voting representation in the US Congress and are not entitled to electoral votes for president. Puerto Ricans living in one of the states, however, may vote. That might explain why disaster relief is so slow to Puerto Rico, she thinks, vaguely remembering reports of conditions after recent hurricanes.

The United States would soon find strategic use for the island beyond warm bodies for its armed forces. Forward-thinking Franklin Roosevelt toured Puerto Rico in 1919, before he became president, and saw immediately the tactical advantage of an air and naval base between the Puerto Rican islands.

The islands lay precisely on the oil and supply lanes upon which the United States was deeply dependent, making them vulnerable to attack. Just as importantly, a US defensive void in the Caribbean opened the possibility of adversaries installing their own base within striking distance of mainland America. Sensible though it was, Roosevelt's early pleas for a stronghold on Puerto Rico, spilling into Vieques, fell upon ears deafened by war weariness.

Soon, though, global aggressions and the dominance of sea warfare elevated interest in the United States' outlying holdings in the Pacific and Atlantic. Roosevelt, now imbued with presidential power, signed an order creating the Roosevelt Roads naval base, affectionately known as "Rosy." The order commandeered a large portion of eastern Puerto Rico as well as the western third of Vieques and its smaller sister island, Culebra.

And thus began a new era on Vieques.

———

The assault began immediately. As with its Spanish oppressors, under US rule the island was drawn and quartered, this time to achieve multiple, sometimes conflicting military goals: to fortify the larger Roosevelt Roads Naval Station; to protect US shipping lanes from German U-boats; to prevent an Axis presence in the Caribbean, close enough to the mainland to be an attack threat; and to act as an emergency base for Allies' naval units in the event their native bases fell to the Nazis. Roosevelt Roads aspired to be the largest military base in the world, spanning three islands, and envisioned as the Pearl Harbor of the Atlantic.

Remaining sugarcane plantations, pristine beaches, small farms, forests, and delicate lagoons were destroyed to make way for the base. Large gashes were hacked into the mountains for ammunition magazines. And the gentle peoples who had long tended and lived in harmony with the land were unceremoniously evicted.

Soldiers simply arrived with guns and heavy construction equipment and informed the residents it was time to leave. Humble patchworked homes that had stood for generations, garden plots with fruits still on the vine, gates, and chicken coops were all razed, often while evicted families watched. Some thoughtful soldiers paused the destruction long enough to allow families to scavenge the wreckage for wood or tin.

What could be carried could be taken. What couldn't was bulldozed. Left behind were life-sustaining farm plots and gardens, chickens and goats, and access to mangroves, lagoons, and familiar seashores. The delicate courtship between island and Jibaro of tending and sowing and reaping and flourishment was abruptly thrown into turmoil.

Jibaro were assigned lot numbers in resettlement tracts in the arid central region of the island, with far less fertile ground and limited access to lagoons and beaches. The exchange granted neither ownership nor rental rights, with the understanding that a similar resettlement was possible, perhaps probable.

Frantic construction of the base commenced at the same pace as escalating tension between the Axis and the Allies. Construction and service jobs on the island were plentiful and well paying. US-backed social services and food subsidies were introduced, shifting the means of survival from plantations and the land to the military and the government. The Jibaro's forced sacrifice brought some rewards.

Until, less than two years after construction abruptly began, it abruptly ended. As the world witnessed American pride tattered and its heart's blood splattered on the shores of Pearl Harbor, so, too, did it see the vulnerability of consolidating military assets into large bases. The grand plan for Roosevelt Roads was scrapped alongside the United States' commitment to remain neutral in the new world war.

The end of the massive building effort left the Jibaro without plantation wages, without the fertile land and protein-rich seafood that had sustained their ancestors, without homes, and without the fleeting construction and service jobs.

The defilement of the island had only just begun.

CHAPTER 7

"God took *mami* young. But God never takes without giving, and he gave us my sister, Rosie. Rosie raised all eleven of us. And finished school. And took care of Pa. He was sick for a very long time."

Knowing she is in hospice care, Ambrose has expected Philomena to be frail and sickly. The woman who greets her at the door of the small, cozy bungalow set in the rolling farmland just outside Philadelphia is robust and full of life. Ambrose assumes she has the wrong address and looks from the woman to the house number to the Puerto Rican protest flag hanging from the porch in a bit of confusion. Philomena welcomes her with a belly laugh and a vivacious hug.

Proud African cheekbones elevate her face, refusing to bow to seven decades of gravity. Gray filaments stream through her silken cacao hair. Sparks of playfulness counterbalance the weight of lava-rock eyes. She is small and plump, descended from the steady stock of Spain, with the broad forehead and caramel-red skin of Taino, radiant against a sunflower blouse. She carries with her the story human, her aura dancing to the drummed rhythms of ancestors and singing with the gods of plow. Her spirit knows how ancient edifices came to be and giggles at our flum-moxed modern attempts to puzzle them.

A rosary of childishly gaudy beads hugs her neck before diving joyfully toward her bosom, disappearing in her cleavage. One imagines the pendulum ends in a scandalous salsa of crucifix and flesh. She wears a brightly colored patchwork apron with starched ruffles and sagging pockets.

Rich coffee steams away the October chill from Ambrose's hands as she follows Philomena's bustling from her perch on a wooden kitchen chair. Philomena's coffee is exceptionally good, earthen, nutty, solid without overpowering, bold without bitterness.

Ambrose can't pinpoint what Philomena is doing. Broths simmer on the gas stovetop, but she isn't exactly cooking. Pots and pans are shifted, but she isn't exactly cleaning. Herbal plants sprouting from old teapots are being tended, but she isn't exactly gardening. Philomena's choreography is beautiful and hypnotic and purposeful but indiscernible.

Philomena places in front of Ambrose a delicate porcelain plate with a large, flaky pastry rich with cream filling and drizzled with honey. Ambrose knows interviewing technique enough to never refuse an old woman's cooking and calculates in her head how many miles of dreaded running the rich pastry will cost.

"*Pastelito de guayaba.*" Philomena brushes off Ambrose's concerns, though Ambrose has yet to voice them. "It's guava. Fruit. Is good for you!"

Ambrose smiles and tears off a piece of pastry. It is heavenly—soft and rich and delicate, a mix of refreshing citrus and buttery phyllo-like dough. It is worth a mile or two. The rich coffee and softly crusted silken cream allow her senses to ease into the place.

Strong colors and wild patterns in a mismatched tapestry flow across the cluttered kitchen, creating a deeply harmonious sense of contentment. Posh spas, so elegantly styled in monochromatic schemes of gray, outfitted with muted artwork and motorized fountains drizzling recycled water over silicone rocks, could benefit from the calming chaos of Philomena's kitchen.

"Your nephew, Rick, who is generously paying me to write your family's story, told me your father died of cancer."

"*Sí*, a cruel death. For him. For us. He lingered—unable to live, unable to die—for years." She pauses, crosses herself, reaches for a tin can on a high shelf, and, as she continues to talk, pulls from it a coin, which she places in an engraved copper bowl at the feet of a beautifully adorned santo, the wooden statue's dark face reflecting power and peace.

Philomena catches Ambrose's quizzical smile. "Americans, you bury your dead and let them lie. We bury bodies but still walk with the spirits of ancestors. Loa, our saints, allow this when we acknowledge them. Ignore the Loa or ignore your ancestors, and they will ignore you."

Then, without contradiction, she turns from conjure to Catholicism.

"God does not give trials without reason. The trials he sends prepare us. Rosie, Rick's mother, my sister—she took care of our father. And she took care of us. She began to see God's plan for her lay in caring for others. She became a nurse. She became a mother," proclaims Philomena, certain the outcome proves God's wisdom.

"She took care of ten kids, plus herself and an ailing father, and finished school all while still a teenager?" wonders Ambrose. "What a saint."

"Never an angry word," says Philomena, nodding. "She went to nurse college in America after she married Robert, Rick's father."

Ambrose saw her opening. "Robert was military?"

"Oh, *sí*. Those handsome American soldier boys. So strong. Carefree. Always smiling. What girl could resist, no?" Philomena pauses her bustling, turning to look directly at Ambrose with a mischievous grin. "Ahhhh, but you have affection for a fighter's smile."

Ambrose startles, flashing to Marcus's quirky grin, thrown off balance by the old woman's uncanny intuition.

"Is good. His smile is scarred. Scars are wisdom. If you live without scars, you have not lived! You lust after him because of his scars, not despite them, and that is pure." She giggles impishly at her pronouncement before becoming serious. "Love your own scars, too, *mija*."

Ambrose is touched by Philomena's use of the Spanish endearment bestowed upon close female friends.

Philomena returns to her indiscernible bustling and continues. "Robert was good to Rosie. Good to us. He waited for her. He waited for us to grow up, for us not to need her anymore before they left the island. Then, one by one, they sent for us."

"So the military coming had a happy ending for you?"

"The military brought endings and beginnings, happy and sad. At first, we had to leave our homes. But we were hopeful. Viequenses are hopeful, always hopeful," she says wistfully.

"You literally got kicked out of your homes? Did you protest?"

"Protest is a luxury that comes with power. No power. No protest. And protest what? We—the Jibaro who worked the land—didn't *own* land. Cane planters owned the island, then the navy owned the island. They let us live on plots of it, tend it, keep what we grew, but never is the land ours. Vieques is our mother, but our mother is a slave."

"You lived on land you didn't own? Like renting?"

"Not renting. Squatting. And not homes like this," she says, waving her hand, "solid and brick and permanent. Our homes were of wood and tin and cloth. Easy to move."

"Still, they could just kick you out of your wood and tin homes?"

"Not could. Did. Soldiers came one day with their official letters and guns and open trucks bigger than we had ever seen. They told us how important our land was, how important our sacrifice was to the war effort. They needed our land to defeat the evil Nazis. We felt important. We felt American. We had only been citizens—well, *almost* citizens—for a very short time." Ambrose scribbles in the margins of her notebook.

"America, she would care for us. It would be better than the plantation owners. So we packed our pots and our santos, a few tools, all the boards and tin we could fit in the big trucks, and they drove us to new, borrowed land." She laughs, remembering.

"It was a very long trip for a few miles! The Americans' big trucks were too wide to get through the forest trails. The soldiers cussed and dented their truck trying to force their way through. Why would those Americans bring such big trucks to such a tiny island?" She shakes her head, speaking as one would of a petulant, though favored, child.

"We tried not to laugh at them. We didn't want to hurt their feelings. We jumped down from that big truck with our machetes and hacked through noni and tamarind so their big trucks could get through and take us to our new, borrowed land!"

Her face grows sad.

"But they would not let us gather the fruit or the leaves or the roots from the cuttings. They said they didn't have time. I did not understand. Still, I do not understand. What good is time without food or herbs or roots?" She sighs, shifting the rosary on her chest.

"The Americans herded us like goats back into their big trucks. They seemed angry, and we could not understand why. We tried to help. No one talked as we drove away. We just watched the sweet fruits of Vieques laying in the road to rot."

She thinks for a moment.

"I hope the animals ate it."

"Did you get to your new borrowed land?" Ambrose prompts gently.

"We did. And, for a while, the Americans brought with them more than handsome boys. They brought jobs! The navy wanted to build a seawall to Puerto Rico, so they hired us. We worked all day, all night, pulling rocks from the island's ground and dumping them in the ocean. And we were paid. Money for everyone!"

"And you could buy your own land and build brick houses?" smiles Ambrose.

"No. Land was never for sale. And no one will build brick houses on land that is not theirs. So the wood and tin houses stayed. But for a short spell, the seawall gave us food and chocolate and very fine clothes!"

Philomena refills Ambrose's coffee mug and, satisfied with the productiveness of her bustling, settles into a rickety chair at the kitchen table. She brings with her a fat, steaming mug for herself and a small flask. She pours liberally from the flask into her own mug and offers it to Ambrose with a gesture and quizzical look. Ambrose raises her eyebrows, tilts her head, and gives a slight shrug. Philomena spikes Ambrose's coffee without comment and stirs both mugs with a small pewter spoon whose delicate handle bears a large painted emblem—the kind of souvenir spoon displayed on a treasured rack that hung in Ambrose's grandmother's dining room. She could have sworn her grandmother had that exact spoon.

"All old ladies have these spoons!" Philomena says. Ambrose is once again thrown by the woman's clairvoyance and unable to recover before Philomena continues. "Then one day the navy changed their mind. No more seawall."

"Before it was done?"

"Many things were done. The jobs were done. The money was done. The mining was done. Deep scars crisscrossed our island, left open. Still open. Cut and wasted. And we did it. Vieques, our mother, wounded by her own children for a few pennies. Just like the fruits laying to rot in the road. But no, the seawall was never done."

"So much wasted money."

"America wastes much more than money. Our brothers, Juan and Sweet Javier, were wasted. Juan joined the military in those early days—so hopeful and full of adventure and travel and romance," she sighs. "Juan was killed at the Battle of Tarawa. He did not have to die. That battle should have been easy and quick, but the Americans attacked the island without knowing its tides. They trapped their own soldiers between an open beach and armed cliffs. Slaughter. A waste. They sent Juan home with a fine American flag, and the military paid to have him buried at the fancy cemetery in Isabel Segunda."

"And Javier?"

"Sweet Javier. He joined after Tarawa, after Juan died. We don't know what happened to him. He just never came home. They told us he was KIA. That is all. Never did we know where or how or have a body to vigil or wake or commit unto God. Just emptiness. It is comfort to know that Sweet Javier had not a sin to cleanse. His soul was already heaven pure, even without the rite. We carved his name with Juan's."

Ambrose sips her coffee, preparing for the pungent aftertaste of hard alcohol. Instead, she is met with a smooth, seductive richness. She only knows it is liquor from its lulling warmth.

"Do you visit?"

"*El vaivén.* Everyone leaves Vieques. Everyone comes back. It is not visiting, just following the tides. The tides drift away from Vieques, but the tides always drift back to Vieques. *Boricua.*"

"*Boricua*?"

"*Boricua.* It means love of Vieques, attachment to her, to her beauty, her softness, her people, her ways, her foods, her smell. Vieques is not our land; she is our kin." She sighs and drinks from her fat mug before continuing.

"Yes, for Vieques, Americans coming had beginnings and endings. Some happy, some sad. We lost Juan and Sweet Javier and land. We gained Robert and passage to America. Many young men joined the army or navy. Many young women married handsome American soldiers."

"And more jobs?"

"No more jobs on Vieques after the seawall."

"What about roads and housing and PXs on the bases? Surely there were jobs—construction, cooking, cleaning?"

"Not for us. The bases were very secret. Shhhhh. We couldn't be trusted on base." She smiles in imitated secrecy. "We went on base only to see doctors. And that was the special MEDCOM building—away from the others, near the little airstrip."

Ambrose's ears perk. "Your doctors were on base?"

"*Sí.* The navy was better than the plantation owners. In some ways, they took very good care of us. Everyone on the island saw the doctors every six months, females every three months."

"Every three months? Even when you weren't sick?"

"*Sí*. The navy would send their big trucks and take us all. They gave us bags of bread and rations and sometimes chocolate."

"Did your mother see the doctors on base when she was sick?"

"*Sí*. Papa too. Everyone every six months, females every three months," she repeats as if it were a long-ingrained mantra.

"What on earth did they do every three months?"

"Took blood. Peed in a cup. Listened to our heart and our lungs. Asked embarrassing questions. My sisters and I would giggle every time they asked if we had sex. We dared each other to ask the handsome doctors if they were interested!"

Something in Ambrose's sight blurs, then clears to a vision far too crisp to be her own, and an odd smell of roasting coffee beans and honey overcomes her.

Ambrose flashes vividly on fresh pigtailed girls, huddled, whispering, giggling, bouncing in the back of an imperial military truck charging reckless through the hacked pathways of virgin forests. The smell of dewy rain forest mixed with gasoline fumes makes her heady and confused. Ambrose shakes out of the vision and glances suspiciously at her spiked coffee.

"Were they the doctors who diagnosed your mother with TB?"

"I suppose. I was young, but I do not remember any other doctors. I know they gave her pills that made her sleep when the coughing got bad."

"Did they talk about sending her to one of the TB sanitoriums on Puerto Rico?"

"No, thank Santa Marta! Before the navy came, sometimes people with coughing sickness would be sent to the big island. They would come home many months later, in a coffin. We do not trust Puerto Rico. We want our people with our people. Even when they are sick. Especially when they are sick. MEDCOM gave her pills and sent her home where she belonged."

"Every three months?"

"Every three months."

"And none of the rest of your family became ill?"

"With coughing sickness? No."

"What about other families?"

"Some had coughing sickness too. They cared for their people. MEDCOM gave them pills. They stayed with their families. All the same."

"But that pattern doesn't fit the epidemiology of tuberculosis."

"Vieques is not America, with big cities and closed houses. Your science works in your world. Vieques is closer to the world God created. His rules still rule in Vieques," she says with the finality of faith that Ambrose knows is pointless to question. And perhaps because of the lulling concoction beckoning in the thick mug, Ambrose suddenly feels like the known rules of the universe, in fact, do not apply—not in Philomena's kitchen and not on Vieques. Theorems and science simply do not apply to those particular coordinates, on that particular island, in that particular ocean, on this particular planet, in this particular galaxy. To Ambrose, at least in this moment, the existence of alternate realities is viable, even logical. Cocooned in that world Ambrose stays, time obliterated and reality softened.

Ambrose came expecting righteous anger at the military's egregious sins. Instead she found a watery-hued mix of love and sadness and resignation blending together, blurred and impressionistic, brushed on a richly saturated backwash of deep-colored *Boricua*.

She stands at the entryway, reluctant to leave, digging through her bag to find her glasses.

"I can never find my glasses. And I can't see two feet in front of me without them."

"Your eyes are not bad, *mija*. God just built them to see different things."

Ambrose, moved by the quaint, kind wisdom, hugs Philomena.

"Thank you. My eyes see why Rick is so fond of you. You know he calls you his bonus mom."

"God chose not to bless me and my Charlie with children."

For the first time in a conversation heavy with emotional topics,

Philomena becomes visibly emotional. Even Philomena's faith is no comfort to this mother's heart left childless. To Ambrose this is yet another cruel contradiction—a woman so deeply nourishing left barren.

"I am so sorry."

"It is a punishment from God for . . . something." Philomena bows her head in shame. "Something that happened on Vieques when I was very young. I must remember that and bear his punishment well."

Philomena wipes her eyes with her plaid apron, her rosary shifting once more, hugging a bit closer. "We longed to have many children. I especially wanted a boy to name after Sweet Javier. But we must accept God's will and give love to every child. Rick is my child. My nephews and nieces are my children. My neighbors are my children. All the children of Vieques are especially my children. And you, Ambrose, you are my child."

Ambrose feels the compliment deeply and marvels that her immediate affection and strong attachment to this woman are mirrored in her newfound friend. She has always found it difficult to gauge another's emotions and has misread often enough to guard her own.

"Let your heart heal, my child. Give grace. Your boy with the scarred smile, believe him when he tells you he is not your enemy."

Ambrose doesn't understand the reference, but enough of the mystical has been transfused in the warm glow of the past few hours that she takes the woman's declaration as gospel. She pulls the prescription shades out of her purse, preparing to drive. Philomena points at the glasses.

"Remember, Ambrose. Your eyes are not flawed; they are just made to see different things. You will go to Vieques, and you will come to know this. Go to the graveyard. Spirit has a message for you. Don't waste it, *mija*."

CHAPTER 8

She pauses a moment behind the steering wheel, wondering if the coffee concoction will earn her a DWI. She finds she is not intoxicated, at least not in a way measured by a Breathalyzer. She is content, soothed, softened, quieted. More rare, she feels disarmed, and comfortable being disarmed. She feels safe.

The drive back to the city from its suburbs is all highway—long, flat, straight, repetitive—just what she needs to ease back into a world ruled by science rather than Philomena's God and santos.

A white, late-model Challenger passes her, and she bristles. She has a thing for Challengers. More than a "thing," less than an obsession. Maybe a "thang." And she is certain Challengers shouldn't be white.

"Another waste, my dear Philomena," she sighs to herself.

Her dashboard Bluetooth chirps.

Snap from 2nddegreeMarcus.

ur being irrational

Her heart pounds and her body salivates, obeying his Pavlovian bell.

2nddegreeMarcus: *id apologize but i dunno even know what for* 🙍 *we never had that conversation maybe we should?*

She doesn't answer. She feels trapped. Paradoxically, the more she tries to guard herself, the more exposed she becomes. She knows the longer she is quiet, the more difficult it will be to explain why she can't respond. She simply can't find her voice.

"Peopling," her term for others' ability to connect, comes so easily to him. Everyone loves Marcus. He is quick witted, sardonic, strong, confident, attractive, successful. He toys with dozens of women who compete for his attention on cue. She doesn't know how to play that game. She doesn't know how to be coy and casual, as flippant and flirtatious as girls who spell their names in cutesy ways and spend hours at the spa. Serious and directed, she is not that complex. She simply wants him—only him. But she is not ruled by her emotions and is determined not to lay herself at the feet of someone who would make sport of the gift of her trust and her soul.

Her feelings for Marcus and her inability to act on them create a conundrum from which she sees no escape, other than to pull back and learn to live with the clichéd hurt of unrequited love. Maybe occasionally masturbating, fantasizing about licking every one of his scars, the Celtic runes on his broad chest hovering over her, the animal smell of cologne mixed with fresh-from-the-fight sweat, her sparce lipstick smudged from having his cock deep in her throat, his strong hands entwined in her hair from behind, pulling her back until she swallows him . . .

She begins to shift in her car seat just as the phone rings, and the dash reads "Kev."

She composes herself and mutters, "Saved by the bell . . .

"Hey, cuz," she answers.

"It wasn't TB."

"I know. What was it?"

"Have no idea. But it was decidedly not tuberculosis. Qualifying this as an unofficial review—small sample group, inconclusive, incomplete records—I am not saying what I'm about to say to you. Clear?"

"Understood. I am not asking you to eat pickles here, Kev. I'm just asking for the impression of pickles."

"Well played. The records indicate classic TB symptoms: dry cough, coughing up blood, weight loss. But contrary to TB, which presents in both lobes of the lungs, seventy-two percent of these patients show invasions of only one lobe."

"It really wasn't TB."

"In my opinion, and based on limited evidence, no."

"Any guesses as to what it was? Could it have been misdiagnosed? Strain of pneumonia?"

"No. None of that fits. The closest known disease I can find is mesothelioma."

"The asbestos thing with the bad legal commercials?"

"Yes, the asbestos thing with the bad legal commercials. It matches in symptoms—TB-type cough, weight loss, lumps under the skin of the chest, but affecting only one lobe of the lung. But mesothelioma takes decades to surface. Most of the patients in this sampling were too young to have developed mesothelioma, even if conditions were ripe for it. This disease's progress was far too aggressive to be mesothelioma."

"Was it contagious?"

"Based on the limited data, no. There is little correspondence in proximity or exposure. And, Ambrose, there are far more disturbing details here."

She grips the steering wheel more firmly.

"Vieques *knew* TB."

"Right. Would you say the island was scathingly familiar with TB?" she queries.

"Scathingly? No. I would never use the world scathingly. But I would classify them as familiar. A patient with TB in your 1940s Vieques would find themselves with medical staff far more familiar with TB than those walking into a modern-day American hospital, and probably receive more appropriate diagnosis and treatment."

"Well, that should have been good for our patients in 1940s Vieques, right?"

"Only they didn't follow TB protocol. The doctors didn't send supposedly contagious patients to available sanatoriums on Puerto Rico. They sent them back to their homes."

"I just talked with someone who lived through it, Kev. They didn't *want* their family going to those sanitoriums. They may have simply refused that treatment."

"But, Ambrose, they weren't even given the option. A patient's refusal of recommended treatment would be especially noted to protect the physician."

"Meaning?"

"Meaning one of two things, both of which are alarming. Either the doctors believed those patients had TB and failed to follow recommendations in the best interest of the patient and to mitigate community spread. Or, more likely given the island's familiarity with TB, the doctors who diagnosed, treated, and signed the death certificates naming TB as the cause of death had to have *known* those patients didn't die from TB. And something else. Did you compare the demographics of the patients?"

"No."

"Ambrose, every one of these deaths were local females between the ages of thirteen and forty-five."

She pauses enough to absorb.

"And all were attended by same physician, Dr. Ira Caldwell, at the same clinic."

"MEDCOM on the base?"

"Yep. MEDCOM on the base."

"I think I need a trip to the library, and maybe to the pristine beaches of Vieques."

CHAPTER 9

She reviews the highlighted fragments of the military reports she has spent hours poring over in the research room at the library—"napalm," "acids," "toxic waste," "irradiated," "unexploded ordnance of unknown origin," "additional unspecified materials," "unidentified substances," and "unknown fiber-like substance"—and mutters to herself, "Jesus, they don't even know."

Her laptop's backlit screen shows a Google map centered on Vieques, with much of the eastern and western portions of the island marked "National Wildlife Refuge." Clicking links reveals photographs of shallow azure waters, crisp sand beaches, and photoshopped couples silhouetted by glittering waves of gold, widening toward horizons swollen with pregnant, setting suns. Pop-up ads claim the pristine beaches of Vieques are rated among the world's best.

"How can something so contaminated be so beautiful?" she mumbles, shaking her head.

She laughs out loud at an advertisement for tours of the bioluminescent bays. "Good God, it actually glows like the Springfield Nuclear Power Plant. Only things missing are Mr. Burns and a three-eyed fish."

Another click conjures a hammocked couple napping under a dense tropical canopy with the words "Ecotourism at its purest on Vieques!"

"Ecotourism? Among arsenic and uranium and napalm? And unknown substances? What the fuck?"

She removes her glasses and rubs her eyes. For hours she has been flipping between the death certificates, her laptop, heavy books, handwritten ledgers, and an ancient microfiche machine.

She sighs heavily, exasperated to the point of talking aloud to herself.

"I can find a hammock and kayak tour on Vieques. But I can't find evidence of a MEDCOM clinic or a Dr. Ira Caldwell associated with MEDCOM. No MEDCOM clinic—no clinic at all, not even for the soldiers. Nothing. Officially, there was no clinic where men could be seen every six months, females every three months."

Head in her hand, she only slowly realizes someone has entered the room. For a moment she thinks he is a mirage of her exhausted mind.

"Thought I might find ya here."

Marcus's large frame, so graceful on the mat, is awkward and clumsy and utterly charming in the small, stuffy room of dusty books and old computers. To her overburdened mind, the sight of him is surreal, a pleasant dream. Her heart warms, an ash-gray, long-smoldering desire for him kindles to crimson. She smiles with seduced poppy-field languor.

Nervous and uncomfortable, he scans the musty room. "Jesus, ya really like this place?"

He picks up a copy of *Island at War: Puerto Rico in the Crucible of the Second War*, rifles a few pages, sets it back down.

"You're really into this World War II thing, huh?"

She doesn't answer. She sits leisurely in the corner while he stalks the room, her head still cradled in her hand, her gaze caressing his movements, languid with longing. So mesmerizing is the sound of his voice, she barely comprehends his words. She really doesn't need to—he has already won by coming for her, for meeting her here, in her arena. She is his.

He stops his purposeful stalking, throwing pretense aside, and turns to her, bold and resolute.

"We're gonna have this conversation. Now."

Her head finally leaves her hand, her brows lift, her head puppy-dogs, and her lazy poppy-field smile deepens, lascivious, curious, yearning. Some women might find his directness intimidating. She finds his assertiveness irresistible, alluring. The smoldering desire sparks pyre blue.

Without breaking his deliberate gaze, he pulls a wooden chair directly in front of her and sits on it backward, his expansive build cornering her. He feels her suddenly, drastically shift away, and he misinterprets its cause.

"I know. I'm 'social.' You're not. So fucking what. I have a business to run. I need to be social for that. But I'm here, Ambrose. With you. Now. OK. I'm fucking here."

He is saying everything she wants to hear. But she can't hear it. An overpowering smell of turning seafood makes her nauseous.

The library walls become the solid oak of a large wardrobe. She makes herself ever smaller, thin knobby knees shielding her budding chest. Tucked in the corner, behind a heavy, coarse cloth of Easter purple and gold, she breathes nasal and shallow and tells her heart shhhhhhhhhh. She can feel his presence through the coarse cloth, his large frame cornering her, the nauseous smell of turning seafood close. He has found her.

"What'da ya want from me?" His raising voice still does not reach her.

"I mean that literally. Ambrose, I don't know what ya fucking want. You gotta tell me." He pauses. "For a writer, you're so goddamn hard to read."

The Easter purple folds on itself until it is close to a deep plum wine, occasionally jettisoned with mesmerizing floats of gold that her eyes follow, hovering and distant.

"Ambrose, I only have so much fucking patience."

Marcus can't be here in the plum-wine closet with the drowsy, slumbersome floats of gold. He can't know she is here. No one can know. Especially not him. He can't know what a naughty little slut she is. He can't know she was never too young, that she was born for it. Some girls are. He can't know she is dirty and used and broken. He can't know she is too weak. Her parents will be so disappointed in her. They won't love her anymore. And someone like him—he will never love her.

Seized with panic, she bolts for the door, leaving him, her research, her phone, her wallet, everything.

Ironically, she finds a supply closet and curls into a small ball, waiting for the panic to pass. When it does, she cries deep and lonely and very quietly.

After a while, she pulls herself up, ashamed and embarrassed. Now she will have to find a new gym, just as she was getting comfortable there. She hates having to constantly start over again every time she fucks up. She returns sheepishly to the room, looking around the corner to make sure he is gone.

He is, and she is overwhelmed with competing feelings of relief and heartbreak. She gathers her research hastily, rubbing her sniffles on her sleeve, absentmindedly jamming papers into her bag. She needs to leave, needs to get out quick, lest anyone see her. She is sure people can tell. She is sure they know.

She stops when she sees a brass key anchoring a note scribbled in a messy blocked hand. "Key to club. Come anytime . . . mean it. Here when you are ready."

She collapses into the chair, hugging his note, and cries for a long time.

When the wave of emotion fades, she picks up her phone, slides up the yellow ghost, and does something much braver than sparring a six-foot-two-inch, 240-pound opponent.

She Snaps him.

KickboxAmbrose: *I'm so fucked up*

2nddegreeMarcus: *i know* 😊 *ready to talk?*

KickboxAmbrose: *No*

2nddegreeMarcus: 😌

KickboxAmbrose: *Sometimes when I can't talk, I can still write.*

2nddegreeMarcus: *ok well i mean i can read, so write*

Tears roll down her cheeks. He has no idea how his simplicity feels to her. Not having to explain, not having to be rational where there is no rationality.

CHAPTER 10

She senses more than sees Will through the glass of the downtown Philly office building. Through a lifetime of poor vision, she has learned to recognize people, especially those most familiar, by their shape, their gait their clothes and hair, their countenance, their aura. Even with glasses on, sensing is more accurate than sight. She observes him a moment. He leans on a coffee bar in the lobby, lowering himself enough that he can gaze adoringly at the attractive barista as if captivated by her. Occasionally he breaks his adoration to hawk the lobby. This scenario is a microcosm of his personality: desperately trying to convince everyone they are the only one.

Ambrose pulls herself upright with a deep inhale, steels herself for the madness of narcissism, and enters. Predictably, when he sees her, he also straightens, taps the coffee bar with a quick have-to-go-to-work smile at the young barista, and hurries toward Ambrose. Will is not particularly handsome, though perhaps he once was. Balding, with heavy jowls and a bent nose and the sad air of a man who still sees lost youth reflected in the mirror, he has the practiced facade of a disarming and charming bumbler. His suit is cheap and disheveled, formal enough to convey effort but casual enough to make him approachable.

He is all smiles and charm.

"Hi," he greets her sheepishly. "I'm really glad you're here. Came down to escort you, m'lady. Just in case ya forgot how to get to your favorite editor's office."

At the elevator, he steps aside, guiding her into the ornate conveyor, his hand grazing the small of her back with an oiled veneer of chivalry. She catches him in the mirrored elevator wall glancing back to the barista with a quick wave of his other hand. One hand on the small of her back, one hand waiving to the barista. Another reflection of who he is. She recoils from his touch.

Alone as the elevator door closes, his attention engulfs her. "I, uh, I wore the tie you picked out. Remember that?" he says, nervously toying with his plaid tie. She doesn't remind him that she had chosen the steel-blue tie. He bought the plaid one instead, somehow internalizing the lie that it was her choice. His hand grazes his sparce head. "Brushed my hair for ya."

Her knowing silence makes him uncomfortable. "Are you gonna say anything? Might be a long meeting if ya don't."

"Why did you come down to meet me? A coffee girl isn't quite enough to have you make the trip. Must be something else. What or who are you avoiding?"

"Nothing. No one. I just . . . like I said, I'm just happy you're here," he stammers. "It's been so long, and . . . I'm glad you're here. She's just a sweet college girl."

Ambrose smirks. "You don't have to justify your new supply to me."

"Why do you say it like that? Supply. It's vulgar."

"Because you feed off people. *That's* vulgar."

"Still prickly. I like you prickly."

She doesn't respond, her expressionless eyes fixated on the elevator door.

"How's boxing?" he asks, searching for some common ground.

"I know more ways to kill people now."

He retreats, then tries again. His narcissism endows him the admirable quality of tenacity. "Have you bought that Challenger you always wanted yet? Gray, with tinted windows. The Hellcat, right?"

"There's a new one. Hellcat Redeye," she responds flatly.

"Oh. So, a red Challenger now?"

Moved by his mind-numbing stupidity, her eyes leave the elevator door to look at him incredulously.

"No, it is called a Redeye. It is not necessarily red," she sneers.

"Oh. So, still gray with tinted windows?"

"Yes, gunmetal gray with tinted windows," she concedes, breaking into a slight smile.

The elevator doors open to a large, busy office with partitioned half walls.

"Do you want to visit Ang and Donny? Get the band back together?" he asks, emboldened by her smile, however slight, and gesturing past his corner-office door to the open area.

She ignores the gesture and walks directly into his office, passing its comfortable couch to perch on the formal chair across from his desk.

"I do not. I can't even imagine what you've told those people."

He mumbles in self-defense. Her rigidity and directness disarm and anger him. Following her lead, he settles for the formality of his expensive polished leather chair. Sitting on his throne, his balls safely hidden beneath an imposing desk, his composure is restored.

"I think there's been a lot of misunderstandings between us," he says diplomatically.

"Purposeful misunderstandings are lies."

Silence.

"I'm not here to rebuild relationships, Will. I know this is difficult for you to understand, but my being here has nothing to do with you. *Nothing.* I'm here despite you, not because of you. I honestly don't even know why I need to be here—why can't you approve this trip? Surely you have the authority to grant a request so minor as a trip to Vieques in a company this large." She knows questioning his authority will irk him. He likes to convey an image that all is done with his blessing and nothing without it, an image fortified by his propensity to take credit for others' successes and blame others for his failures.

"I will forgive you not knowing that media corporations are rather tight these days, considering you refused my offer of a corner office for less pay, less power, and the grungy view from your apartment," he digs. "How's that working out for you?"

"I love my view," she defends honestly. "And those with true power rarely need to make such effort to show it."

He shrugs arrogantly. "But this particular issue is not one of money. It is of politics. In today's divisive and uncertain world, editorial committee approval isn't enough. An executive committee, led by Mr. Haufmann himself, wants approvals on any investigative reporting on political figures or government entities—foreign or domestic."

"This doesn't involve the current administration or any one person—it is much broader scope and historical. Frankly, it might provide a distraction to the current administration. Did you go through the research I sent? There's an untold story there."

"I did." He nods, pulling out a folder containing printed copies of their email exchange with pages of attachments. "And I can't disagree with you. There might be a story there."

"Might?"

"Ambrose," he sighs. "I know this isn't what you want to hear. It's certainly not what I want to tell you. I shared this with the committee and Mr. Haufmann and pled the case. I don't agree with them, but, Ambrose, for them, it was just a stale story—ran its course decades ago. It's common, or at least public, knowledge—there was a military training base on the island. Mistakes were made. Ugly things happened. End of story."

"A little more than ugly things," she protests. "Sixty years of stealing land to play war games, poisoning the island with substances they can't even identify. Bombed from dusk till dawn every day for decades. Five million pounds of live ordnance exploded every year, Will. And twenty-two million pounds of toxic waste."

She rifles through her own collection of papers and reads from a highlighted page.

"'Toxic compounds, lubricants, acid, arsenic, lead, mercury, cadmium, depleted uranium, napalm, tons of an unknown or unidentifiable substance. Most of these toxins are categorized as persistent, with the ability to bioaccumulate. In the waters, decommissioned ships, drums of waste, and other objects were sunk for targeting and testing. All contaminated with oil, solvents, radioactive shipwrecks, sunken steel barrels containing nuclear waste, and more unidentified compounds. Known quantities of nuclear waste and barrels of unidentified substances remain unaccounted for.' *They lost nukes, Will.*" She looks at him incredulously.

"The key word being 'known.' Nothing new here, oh fairest one. The story's already been told. After a local died in an FA-18 misfire, there was a spectacular uprising shored up by social justice royalty—Al Sharpton, Jessie Jackson, even the pope—the kind of thing that appeals to you."

"Felix Trinidad."

"Who is Felix Trinidad?"

"He's a boxer. From Puerto Rico. He was in on the protests. Same year he beat De La Hoya."

"Oh. Well, that should appeal to you more. Hell, Bobby Kennedy named his kid Vieques—the kid was born while Bobby was serving jail time for his part in the protests. And the pope and Kennedy and your boxer won—they forced the military to stop bombing and turn the base into a wildlife refuge. Happy ending, right? David wins against Goliath?"

"The wildlife refuge wasn't an act of warm, fuzzy restitution. Designating the affected area as a national wildlife refuge means the land is unfit for human habitation. Being such, the military had no obligation to clean it up, bears no future liability, and can deny past accountability. The military's own studies show there is still unexploded ordnance containing mercury, lead, copper, magnesium, lithium, napalm, depleted uranium, and, again, unidentified substances. *This isn't over.*"

"'Their own studies' evidences a commitment to mitigate past damage and take on exactly the accountability you deny exists."

"They acknowledge the substances while denying the consequences." Sifting through the papers once more, she points to another highlighted section and reads: "A study by the World Health Organization showed crabs from Icacos Lagoon are contaminated one thousand times tolerable maximum ingestion dosages of heavy metals known to cause asthma, cancer, and infant mortality." She pulls out another report, citing, "Hair samples show sixty-nine percent of natives are contaminated with cadmium and arsenic and thirty-four percent with toxic levels of mercury." And another: "The island has a twenty-seven percent cancer rate." And another: "Residents of the island who lived through the bombings are at increased risk from vibroacoustic disease."

"The military claims the sample sizes in those studies are too small to be scientifically significant," Will counters.

"There are less than ten thousand natives," she says, voice cracking with exasperation. "If one hundred percent of them had cancer, the military would *still* claim the sample size was too small. That is an indefensible and illogical loophole."

"I know. I hear you. I agree with you. But you know this game, Ambrose. Mr. Haufmann is politically savvy. He has connections to consider, connections that allow him access to information that has helped build the reputation and success of this company. He doesn't like the optics of the story. Now is not the time to resurrect distrust in the military or stoke racial tensions or be seen by political allies as instigating either. My sources tell me the US military is truly trying to do right by that island. They acknowledge hazardous materials and unexploded bombs are still on the island and have conducted extensive studies and publicly designate posted red zones to prevent exposure or accidents."

"Or the red zones are there to guard something else, Will. They've had decades and billions of dollars invested in this cleanup. If the real intent was to neutralize the area, wouldn't there be some progress? Where's all that money gone? It's certainly not going to build hospitals or care for civilians whose cancer was caused by exposure. Something is off, Will."

He pauses. "I'm on your side here. I fought to give you resources to investigate. I will continue to fight for that. Gimme something else—a new angle, some additional research . . . "

She reaches quickly into her backpack and pulls out her laptop and a few manila envelopes, fueled by equal parts anger and a desire for justice. "I have that. It *is* a new angle. Even with all that *is* known and acknowledged, there is more. The discrepancies with TB haven't been explained, and, Will, the doctors knowingly falsified death certificates. The victims of this supposed TB were all females of child-bearing age, and all were treated at the same MEDCOM. Why would that be?"

"I looked into your MEDCOM. There was no MEDCOM on the island. Even the soldiers went to Puerto Rico for health care."

"The people who lived there claim differently. They claim they were seen by MEDCOM doctors every six months, every three months for females."

Will's brow furrows for a moment. Leaning in, he opens the manila envelopes. She mimics his posturing. For a quarter of an hour, they huddle, poring over the reports and data, building on each other's theories, ever closer until they are arched just inside the circled glow of intimacy.

"I've never asked this before, Will. I wanna go after this one," she pleads in a low, almost-whispered voice, raspy with intent and urgency. Her cobalt gaze is momentarily unguarded and pure. He is absorbed by her energy. He is intoxicated by it.

"This is how it should be, Ambrose. I know you feel it, too. We always made a great team."

She snaps to attention, awakened from the spell. She gathers her laptop quickly and rises to go.

"I'll leave the envelopes. Can you make Mr. Haufmann reconsider?"

"Ambrose, you have my word. I'll do my best. And I'll reach out again to my military contacts. See what I can dig up. I've got your back on this. I wanna make things right between us."

Then she is gone. He sits on his throne, balls still tucked under the imposing oak, feeling the room depressurize.

————————

Bolting through the open office, she avoids eye contact with people she once knew. She lowers her chin and rolls her shoulders forward, appreciating how boxing has taught her how to make herself small. She heard through the soured grapevine how Will had planted twisted seeds of gossip that blossomed into egregious lies that only grew because she withdrew and refused to respond. She is still angry at those weak enough to believe him, especially those who whispered about his past deceits and manipulations—often victims themselves. Cowards. She is grateful she has pruned them from her life.

Even with her chin purposefully lowered, she can feel his weighty presence as Mr. Haufmann strides from the elevator doors, entourage in tow. The energy in the room alters: backs straighten; nervous glances dart around the room; the sound of paper shuffling and sudden, purposeful typing replaces casual office chatter. She is not nervous. Fighting has numbed her to intimidation, even when it is sensible to be intimidated. She is on a collision course with the owner of this multibillion-dollar media corporation, and she does not alter her path.

He smiles in recognition, his deep-set crow's-feet curving toward graying temples stunningly offset by a rich Mediterranean complexion. Genuinely fond of her, he rather enjoys the sport of watching managers attempt to manage her. He is glad the job didn't fall to him.

"Ms. Nobel! What a delightful surprise! Pray tell, what could entice you from the comforts of your cozy abode to grace our dull and dreary office?"

"I came to plead my case for going to Puerto Rico—Vieques—to investigate the bogus TB cases. I have new evidence, Mr. Haufmann. If you could just reconsider . . ." she lobbies passionately before registering his confused expression.

"Puerto Rico?"

"Yes, and I have historical data and victim demographics, and . . . "

"I see I have misled you, Ms. Nobel. I'm afraid I'm unfamiliar with a proposal regarding Puerto Rico. Lovely island, though. Such pristine beaches."

A brutal gut punch of realization steals her breath just as Will appears by her side. Slowly, she turns to Will, speechless.

Mr. Haufmann senses the tension and smiles. His success is very much owed to an astute understanding of human relations and when to stay out of them.

"Mr. Narcy, Ms. Nobel has a project from Puerto Rico she wishes you to consider. I'm sure you will give it the utmost consideration and bring it to our next review, where we might take it under advisement. I look forward to it." Then, turning to Ambrose, he says, "A delight, Ms. Nobel. Do visit more often. You are endlessly refreshing."

He fondly touches her shoulder, gives Will a stern look, and strides past, his entourage puppy-dogging behind him.

When she is once again able to speak, her words come in a hoarse staccato, this time forged in white-hot rage as she reddens in embarrassment at her own stupidity. "That's why you met me downstairs. You didn't want me to run into Mr. Haufmann. Because you never gave him the proposal."

"Ambrose, I couldn't. You don't know the whole story. Let me explain."

"And I just gave you all that research. Oh my God, how could I be such an idiot?" She closes her eyes, trying to understand how she didn't see it coming.

"Bigger issues are at play here, Ambrose. Subjects I am not at liberty to talk about. You *need* to trust me on this," he pleads in a harsh whisper, grabbing her arm as she forces past him.

The ferocity of her response causes cube dwellers to abandon their feigned studied indifference and pick up their phones for security. He is trapped, nose bent, smashed against the wall with his arm painfully twisted behind him, her knee lodged into his balls from behind.

"Know this, Will Narcy, and know it with every inch of your miserable fucking being. If you ever touch me again, I will break your fucking arm and shove whatever shriveled, graying testicles you still have up your wrinkled old asshole."

She releases him, bitch-smacking the back of his head. "And you're fucking bald. Everyone knows it. Why don't you?"

She ignores the waiting elevators, finds the stairwell, and flees, strong, rhythmic footfalls ingrained from years of jumping rope and running and ladder drills reverberating all the way down.

"Ambrose, I am protecting you," he calls out to a now-empty stairwell, nursing his arm.

He turns to the stunned, curious office workers. Realizing he needs an explanation, and one that puts him in a good light, he quips, "Hell hath no fury . . ."

The cube dwellers chuckle knowingly, and the tension in the room evaporates.

CHAPTER II

This time her punches and kicks and elbows are not controlled. This time her movements portray exactly what she feels. Fury. Rage. Gone is the smooth voice of Annie Lennox, replaced with violent trash metal. She brawls with her demons in the darkened club, beyond exhaustion, beyond training and form and strategy. Drenched, gasping, her shoulders burning, she is losing.

And this time she does swing when she is startled by a hand on her shoulder. Only one trained, whose body holds the memories of swollen eyes and split cheeks, would slip and catch that savage overhand cross. He does. And he holds it.

"Calm down, killer. Told ya privates are expensive," he quips, smiling that imperfectly perfect smile. But then he sees her—really sees her—face blotched and brined and swollen from a swarthy mix of sweat and tears and snot. Raw. Unfiltered. Vulnerable. Hurt and angry and losing to the demons.

Frozen they stand. Her stance perfection, left glove solid to her jaw, elbow tight, right glove fully extended across his face, shoulder rolled, hips turned, back foot angled on her toes. Her posture is beautifully executed, the refined and practiced form of a trained fighter.

But her beauty in the moment comes from something deeper, something transcendent that would be insulted to be deemed merely beautiful, something untrainable—a primordial femininity buried in the visceral where roller coasters tickle and from which orgasms burst. A rooted place swaddled in pleasing love handles and FUPAs, restrained and shamed and tamed for generations by corsets and latex and endless sit-ups. The tears and sweat and snot don't betray vulnerability but rather badge her as the elemental warrior female challenged and risen and ferocious. She is at once too entrenched and too elevated for language.

He quiets with a short nod and whispers, "OK." He accepts here and now, in the middle of fighting demons, she is unable to speak. She didn't flee. He takes that to mean right now, she is open to him.

He caresses her glove, still caught in his hand, down to his core. She pulls her hand instinctively back, but he holds it solid in place. He turns the worn leather gently, his scarred, knowing hand fondling the tangled knot at the base of her wrist, coaxing the strings upward, deliberate and unhurried.

"Ambrose, when are you going to understand that I am not your enemy?"

Her brows furrow, registering recognition. *Isn't that what Philomena said?* She exhales unconsciously and lowers her left guard, her right still in his hand. Suddenly she is so very tired. New, different, slower tears well.

The laces unravel, and the glove slips off.

CHAPTER 12

Long slighted by Puerto Rico, the United States, and the world, dignified by not even a label on most maps, Vieques will have its revenge. Vieques's tranquil facade, with its coconut-palm-lined beaches, fine sand, and glassine waters, belies a violent birth, the trauma of slavery and ongoing oppression of its people, sustained assaults with the world's most toxic substances, and the certainty of a cataclysmic future. Triggered, it will certainly return to the rage of its youth. The deceptively serene island is rooted deep in an unstable tectonic plate perched treacherously on the Puerto Rico Trench. According to NASA, a mass of gravity lies beneath the Puerto Rico Trench so dense it has a gravitational pull on the ocean, creating a visible dip on the surface and causing navigational instruments to malfunction. Eight hundred miles long, 60 miles wide, the trench encompasses the deepest point in the Atlantic Ocean, Milwaukee Deep. Milwaukee Deep plunges 5.2 miles from Earth's sheath, fingering Her churning molten root, tickling tantric, inviting Her smoldering nectar to rise and fall in prolonged pleasure. In the universe's primordial foreplay, humans are insignificant. The solid ground they strive for, the love and land they die for, is just the veneered surface, dwarfed in the lusted coupling of gods tectonic. Eventually, She will peak.

The trench quakes fifteen times a day, registering a magnitude of least 1.5. When a significant quake happens here, and it is two hundred years in the making, it will generate a catastrophic tsunami. Vieques is on the earthquake's fault line and directly in the path of the inevitable tsunami. Stores of toxic chemicals, unexploded ordnance, storage tanks of nuclear waste, radioactive shipwrecks, and unidentified substances will be unleashed into the world. And then they will remember the name.

She sighs and exits Word, closing the cover of her laptop. She is done writing for the moment. She switches to her phone and Snaps Kev: *At the airport to Vieques*

GermDocK: *Company agreed?*

KickboxAmbrose: *No. Also, related: I think I might not work there anymore.*

GermDocK: *So, you'll be needing* 💰😂

KickboxAmbrose: *Prob'ly*

Then after a moment:

KickboxAmbrose: *Kev, there was no MEDCOM on Vieques. And there was no Dr. Ira Caldwell.*

GermDocK: *Must have been. Death certificates are pathologically accurate*

KickboxAmbrose: *Well, I am going on a pathologically clandestine fact-finding mission.*

GermDocK: *Be careful, cuz.*

KickboxAmbrose: *Love ya*

Double chirps. Sliding the Snap reveals a close-up of broad shoulders and an exaggerated frown topped with tousled curls.

2nddegreeMarcus: *not rolling tonight?*

KickboxAmbrose: *On my way to Puerto Rico*

2nddegreeMarcus: *was i that bad?* 😂

KickboxAmbrose: *I mean, even the best benefit from practicing* 😂

KickboxAmbrose: *If I don't come back, you know the military got me right? Like don't believe them if they tell you* 🦈 *ate me*

2nddegreeMarcus: *Understood*

She pauses.

KickboxAmbrose: *U can have all the parties at Ground Zero you want, knowing I won't walk in on you.*

2nddegreeMarcus: 😒 *at least ur still talking to me*

She pauses, embarrassed anew and unsure.

2nddegreeMarcus: *i think . . . ???*

She gathers her strength and steps in.

For the first time in her life, she sends a heart emoji. It's a fat, sparkly, adolescent pink heart with smaller pulsating hearts floating above. For a moment it feels good, ridiculously childish. Then she panics and rethinks.

"Next I am going to be spelling my name with an 'i,'" she scolds herself. She flips back and deletes the fat pink floaty heart.

2nddegreeMarcus: *too late, already saw it* 😂

She blushes. Is he laughing at her? She closes Snap and decidedly settles into the torn, uncomfortable console chair, arms crossed and pouting like a child. She hates the sway he has over her. Why is she ceding him that power? Is it worth it?

After a moment, she reconsiders and reopens Snap, then switches to Instagram.

She and Marcus are not friends on Instagram or Facebook. She has almost no social media presence, using Snap only to text the few friends she has.

Naturally guarded, she has never understood the desire to share intimate details, or even not-intimate details, with strangers, or even not-strangers. The amount of time and energy people invest in something that gives so little in return astounds her. Liking, loving, swiping, and pressing icons is the lowest common denominator of human interaction.

But she does know how to use the platforms. She isn't quite a stalker, but, being a writer, she is curious about people's behaviors and relationships.

2nddegreeMarcus: *lol don't get all weird*

Does he mean sending pink hearts is weird? Or her sudden silence is weird? She doesn't know. She recognizes an all-too-familiar anxiety rising in her chest.

With time on her hands, amid a swirl of stale travelers and holding a cup of tepid airport coffee that makes her long for Philomena's mysterious concoction, she traces Marcus's Insta impressions. The valley-girl blonde from the club likes all his posts. And he hers. They liberally exchange fire emojis, their most recent exchange from earlier today. Ambrose's heart plummets.

The Barbie-doll blonde isn't the only one. Scrolling down his friends list and following his trail reveals that Marcus cycles through an ever-shifting carousel of women—intensely following for months, suddenly disappearing, then reemerging weeks or even months later.

There is not a single ass pic, bikini shot, workout photo, or duck-faced selfie that he hasn't "liked." He casts a wide net, she thinks, harvesting women indiscriminately to his e-harem. Or perhaps his live harem? His Snap handle is prominently displayed on both his Instagram and Facebook profiles, inviting anyone interested into a nontraceable private conversation.

Social media is not real life, but one can draw reasonable conclusions about real life based on it. As Marcus's online patterns emerge, so, too, does the nausea that accompanies her dawning sense that she's not special to him. She could be anyone. She is just the one female stupid enough to fall for his toying this particular day.

How many women is he sending the exact same Snaps he sent her? How many keys has he given out? How many times has he used the lines she thought were so connective and intimate between them? How could she have been so gullible?

She loves fighting in the ring. She loves the absolute absorption of it—the physical and mental totality. People often subscribe oneness, awareness, and in-the-moment mentality to yoga and massage, and rightfully so. But there simply is no other place where you are more fully present than in the ring with someone trying to knock you down. You feel every inch alive, and nothing else matters. It is forced wholeness. Your body holds every mile and crunch and squat of your training. Your mind holds every trainer, every sparring partner, every hit you have learned from. And you feel it viscerally—every hurt, every anger, every slight, every betrayal is stored deep in your core to be called upon when your muscles and your mind fail you. All that pain is released in round ten when everything else fails.

She loves the aftereffects of fighting too. She loves walking into a room, muscles still taut, bruises still fresh from the night before, to a table full of soft men with manicured nails who believe themselves powerful. She knows what is inside her—she knows her mental and physical limits not because she theorized about them or considered them during a TED talk but because she tested them. She needn't rely on name brands or corner offices or popularity to feel powerful. She lives the saying that those with power rarely need show it. She is almost always the most powerful person in the room, and soft men who assume their power is apparent and unquestioned quickly find she is uninterested and unintimidated.

But she doesn't want to have to fight for a home, for friends, for family, for lovers. She can't focus on the skirmishes of everyday life if she has to keep looking back to see who is in her corner. She would rather have an empty corner than an uncertain one.

2nddegreeMarcus: *not answering?*

Tears welling, chest flushing crimson, and sick to her core, Ambrose clicks the Snap gear button and blocks 2nddegreeMarcus.

CHAPTER 13

Touchdown at San Juan International on a plane full of Puerto Ricans foreshadows the welcome she will find in the Caribbean. She is well traveled. Occasionally, on a flight that has been delayed or experienced high turbulence, passengers will break into applause when the aircraft's wheels safely touch the tarmac. But that is relief applause. The applause of Puerto Ricans returning to their island is different. This is joyful applause. This is reuniting with your schoolmates over drinks. This is lying on a beach on a cushion of sand with a blanket of sun. This is a reunion, a celebration, whose happy sounds will serenade the musky rain forest night and be renewed as dawn gently shakes sleepy azure from the ocean. *Boricua*, Philomena has called it.

A Cessna is the only certain way for non-natives to get to Vieques from Puerto Rico. The ferry prioritizes natives, and, as Philomena has pointed out, the seawall has never been completed.

The Cessna is delayed for reasons suspicious. When the aircraft becomes serviceable, instead of checking in by section as on a traditional flight, the Cessna's porter simply takes attendance by first name, just as Miss Molly does on *Romper Room*.

The five passengers are ordered to turn off their phones. Not just switch to airplane mode, commands the attendant, but fully off. Ambrose has a fleeting thought that mobile phones might interfere with radio signals more on a small Cessna than a 747, but she is quickly disabused of the notion.

"No pictures. Not inside. Not outside," the attendant sternly warns. *It's the camera, not the phone, he is concerned with. That's interesting,* she thinks to herself.

The passengers follow the attendant not to a high-tunneled walkway to transport them to the plane but instead to descend a set of utilitarian stairs—the kind decorated with red carpet for Air Force One—directly onto the tarmac. Once descended from the stairs, they literally walk the tarmac, past the monolithic tunnels of more advanced aviation carriers, smug with little people perched and judging atop their luxurious windowed tunnels. They dodge busy-bee cargo transports, walking for some time before discerning a small aircraft marked with the Cape Caribbean logo hidden behind a fuel truck longer, if not taller, than the plane itself.

An aging pilot wearing a crisp white classic uniform hands the attendant a small bag through an open cockpit window as if he were ordering a drive-through Big Mac. The porter forcefully relieves the passengers of their carry-ons and stores them in the nose of the Cessna before carefully arranging the passengers by weight to balance the small craft. The Cessna resembles a 1972 Lincoln Continental in both size and décor.

The pilot, who resembles Leslie Nielsen in the movie *Airplane!*, orates the safety warnings. He does not offer peanuts, but he does close the cockpit window. He cautions his passengers once more about taking photographs. "Social media," he sighs with a shrug. His weary, resigned demeanor affirms that he doesn't *want* this job—he *needs* this job. Ambrose contemplates what kind of images posted on personal networking sites might cost Leslie Nielsen his job. She sits back uneasily, enduring the bumpy ride in the flying Lincoln, taking in the camouflaged blues of the reefed ocean to her right and, to her left, the ancient, tamed volcanos, softened by a millennium of sun and verdant growth, not unlike a ragged old cowboy softened by a granddaughter's smile.

As much as she has pored over photographs and drawings and satellite images, her first sight of Vieques surprises her. While she can see the entire island tip to tip from the Cessna's rounded window, the land mass is larger than she expected, with imposing lush mountains rising on either end.

Landing is gentle under the pilot's experienced, camera-shy hand. Ambrose thinks fleetingly the pilot was probably a pretty good lay—technically adept, if passionless, and goodness knows there would be no incriminating evidence. The thought reignites ripples of Marcus heartache. The travelers hurriedly descend to an airport smaller than a mainland travel kiosk but without snack machines. Or coffee. Or internet access.

"We ain't in Kansas anymore," Ambrose sighs.

CHAPTER 14

A battered golf cart, one of those comically illustrated *Where's Waldo–*
like tourist maps, and genuinely hospitable people await her at the
airport kiosk. The golf cart rental attendant hands her two keys.
One starts the golf cart. The other unlocks a bike chain that extends
from the cart's seat backing to its steering wheel. The golf cart key will
start any golf cart on the island, as every rented golf cart on the island is
the same make and model and owned by the sole rental company. Only
the bike chain locks are different.

"People were mixing up each other's carts and going to the beach
with the wrong towels," the attendant explains. "So we added bike
chains. Now everyone goes to the beach with their own towels."
Ambrose is charmed to be in a place whose only need for locks is to
prevent beach towel mix-ups.

The cartoon map boldly chronicles the military history of the island in
a cutesy, inappropriate comic font. A tourist attraction of World War II
bunkers that lies on the western portion of the island is marked, as well
as large red warnings for the "restricted" areas that make up the entire
eastern island and parts of the island's western shore. She must look closer

to find the town of Esperanza, where her beachfront guesthouse awaits. Once she's found her destination, she unlocks her bike chain and turns the golf cart toward the island's south coast.

You could be cured of texting while driving if you spent much time on Vieques. It takes all of her concentration to dodge crater-sized pot-holes, Rottweiler-sized iguanas, and "island horses," who are owned but not corralled. She bangs her head on the top of the golf cart during the journey—twice.

After Ambrose arrives a bit rattled twenty minutes later, the guest-house's owner, Lucinda, greets her by name. Lucinda heard the flight had been delayed, and the island had been worried for Ambrose. Not just Lucinda but the island. No anonymity here. The widespread concern is both touching and disconcerting, as unnerving as when Amazon suggests perchance you might care to review their offerings of bagel slicers within a half hour after cutting your finger slicing a bagel.

Research and time with Philomena have prepared Ambrose for a small community interwoven in deep and tribal ways that Main Street America desperately tries to imitate with cheesy festivals and art trails. What Main Street America lacks that is clearly here is mutually dependent survival. Mainlanders no longer need a particular storefront on a particular main street in a particular town—modern America has become a mobile, remote, transient society. Mainland America falsely believes itself fiercely independent, rather than owing that inde-pendence and mobility to a networked infrastructure of health care, education, roads, and services.

Lacking such infrastructure, the people on Vieques still know they *need* each other, and that grants them an endearing humility and earnest concern for the welfare of others. What happens to one happens to all.

There is no hospital, no food bank, no fast food, no Walmart—inter-net, electric, and water are spotty. Only one small grocery store and a convenience store more akin to a campground store than a 7-Eleven grace the main thoroughfare.

Subsistence farming, harvesting, and fishing are mainstays of the local diet, which is incredibly healthful but incredibly vulnerable and weather dependent. People here still live on the land and rely on the ocean and each other, and that necessary interdependence informs the way they value one another.

That lifestyle is felt in Lucinda's welcome. Her greeting is genuine, lacking the deferential, affected style of a Disney hotel or a five-star all-inclusive resort. Island hospitality is more organic than the corporate culture, where guest service is codified and standardized and linked to economic reward. The island's remoteness and the instability of infrastructure make a genuine sense of community an ingrained survival mechanism.

Ambrose reflects that people like Will would never survive in communities based on this kind of authentic mutuality. Ambrose's ideology of attacking the tragedy of abuse by challenging community values rather than "healing" survivors is validated here among the air and light and openness of island life. Shadows on Vieques are playful reflections of palm leaves, ever-shifting pockets of cool relief from the tropical sun. In Philly, the shadows skyscrapers cast are ominous and oppressive, breeding grounds for darkness. There are places in downtown Philadelphia never touched by sunlight.

Ambrose finds her room reflective of the property's owner—pleasant as Lucinda's bright smile. The room is decorated with fresh Caribbean yellows and blues and breezy French doors opening onto a small sundeck overlooking the beach. A small black Virgin Mary santo, similar to the one in Philomena's kitchen, sits on the nightstand, with a small copper dish and some Florida water. She washes, superstitiously cleansing her aura with the Florida water. She consciously opens herself to its healing and protective properties, always willing to absorb the traditions of the land and a little extra protection. She wanders downstairs to the open-air drinkery for a plate of mahi-mahi tacos, served with a crisp citrus island slaw, and watches the Caribbean sun setting over the ocean. Easing into the place, she sips a pink drink from the menu called an Islander, then another.

When the dozen patrons who constitute the dinner crowd disperse, the drinks lubricate a conversation with Lucinda, who is now tending bar. Lucinda is chunky and voluptuous, with sleek, careless hair to her waist, and unbothered by the crow's-feet and forehead wrinkles that announce middle age. Ambrose is captivated by her sensual curves as she works, shaking and turning and pouring in the rhythm of an abundant, life-creating ocean. Even her soft belly, exposed by a sunshine tank top, is inviting.

Being alone now in the bar with her, assuming closing time has arrived, Ambrose clinks her ice as she slurps the last bit of her second Islander and prepares to leave. Instead, Lucinda pulls from beneath the bar an unmarked mason jar with a cloudy liquid and chunks of coconut.

"*Pitorro*," she announces as she pours two shots. "Welcome to Vieques!"

Ambrose settles in with the sweet, strong island 'shine. They speak of small, tentative things the way strangers who think they might like each other do. Eventually, the conversation turns to the hurricane. Most conversations on Vieques eventually turn to the hurricane.

Hurricane Maria dominated mainland news for a cycle or two back in 2017. The Category 5 storm leveled a Puerto Rico already recovering from a similar hurricane just two weeks earlier and a complete financial collapse ending in governmental bankruptcy. Humanitarian relief was sporadic and inconsistent even on Puerto Rico, much less on Vieques. Families lived for months without electricity, running water, and shelter.

The storm lives in Ambrose's mind in the stomach-turning images broadcast around the globe of America's new president visiting a Puerto Rican community leveled by the storm. Impervious to or unaware of the human tragedy, the so-called leader of the free world joyously threw rolls of paper towels to huddled families who had lost children and homes, like a Borgia prince throwing useless trinkets to a defeated, starving people.

She hadn't thought of the shameful scene since, expect perhaps as a reminder of base and blatant narcissism put on display by America's chief executive. But she hadn't thought about the ongoing crisis or the people affected. If she had, she might have known that humanitarian relief barely materialized. The hospital was never rebuilt. Foreign investors left homes and hotels to rot, calculating that rebuilding would be a bad investment. The military that had used the island as a proving ground for decades dispersed canned food and water haphazardly. Even today, warehouses of now-expired food meant for distribution to Vieques are found. The canned goods went unused and expired. Wasted.

"Everything was destroyed. Everything. Homes, schools, boats, the water plant. Chickens and goats died. Mango and avocado and plantain trees gone," said Lucinda, reliving the devastation.

"Before the hurricane, my husband, Carlos, worked at the W, a resort in Isabel Segunda. It wasn't rebuilt. Carlos worked as a lineman fixing the electric after the storm. It was a good job, lots of hours, good pay. But there was no school, no water, no food. I took the kids to live with my brother in Florida. He is so good to us. He gave us a nice home. In America, the kids had school and food and water. We traveled a bit too. Saw New York and Washington and the big Appalachians. But our hearts belong to Vieques. I missed my husband. The kids missed their grandmother and cousins and friends. And we missed the island—eating mangos from the trees, Sundays on the beach after church. We missed it all."

"*Boricua*?" Ambrose asks.

Lucinda is surprised and laughs, correcting Ambrose's pronunciation.

"Yes, *Boricua*. She is our mother."

"It took over a year for schools to reopen. We came home when classes started again. We had money from Carlos's work, and he had experience at the W. This place was selling for almost nothing. We bought it. Spent months fixing it up. My brother was so angry. Said it was a waste, said another hurricane would come. And this time he wouldn't help us when it did."

"How difficult," says Ambrose, trying to imagine what she would do in the same situation.

"I told him to come stay, come eat, come drink. Here. At our home. We love him." She pauses. "I understand. I know he loves us too. And he's right. Another hurricane will come. But I don't want disasters to guide my life. I want to be guided by the life that happens between disasters.

"This." She waves toward the soft sand beach, so close to the open-air bar, with a few sun-bronzed children playing chase in the gentle surf, calling to fisherman docking their small boats. "To me, this is life. This is how I want to raise my children. This is how I want to grow old. This is how I want to live. This is how I want to die."

Ambrose nods, takes a cautious sip of the potent local consolation, and watches the shrilling children playing in the gentle surf. Chunky preteen girls are testing their budding femininity in revealing bikinis. They swagger, exaggerated and unsure, along the familiar shallow shoreline, water lapping at their feet, luring them into a vast unknown ocean.

Ambrose has a pang of nostalgia for the neighborhood kids she grew up with, the ones who met at the basketball court and stole liquor from parents' cupboards and flashed each other on dares and hunted ghosts in the woods.

This island is a neighborhood. Not a tourist destination. Not a military post. Not a little sister to Puerto Rico. A neighborhood.

Lucinda's wisdom, her strength, this island, this potent 'shine, and maybe the mystic properties of the Florida water give Ambrose room for introspection. Will Ambrose want to live and die where she is? What would she do if she could do anything? Would she open her own ghostwriting company? Finish her first novel? Train to fight pro? Learn to fuck Marcus knowing he was fucking others? Move to a little cottage on a lake? Get a dog? She would definitely get a Challenger. Gray, with tinted windows. What is stopping her? Except the fact that now she doesn't have a job. Or money. Or family.

Or maybe she can ask these big life questions, and find the answers, precisely because she now has no job, no money, no family. Where is Ambrose's Vieques?

"*Boricua*," says Ambrose, cheering and, this time, getting the pronunciation closer to correct.

"*Sí, Boricua, mami*," laughs Lucinda, clinking her glass.

CHAPTER 15

She wakes early to a cacophony of animals saluting the sun, head throbbing from *pitorro*. She lies in the comfortable bed, content and warm, trying to distinguish their songs. Roosters, certainly, but they can't all be roosters. She doesn't think monkeys live on the island. Frogs? Birds? Do iguanas sing?

By 6:00 a.m. a peach-sherbet dawn has quieted the morning serenade and warmed the island into the mideighties, offering a refreshing breeze. Perfect weather will last well into the night. Ambrose has always assumed the phrase "island time" meant slothfulness. Now she understands there is simply more consistent daylight in the Caribbean, requiring less planning. One can paddleboard in equal comfort at 6:00 a.m. or noon or 2:00 p.m. or 6:00 p.m. The frantic, urgent hyperscheduling of city life is superfluous here, where day arrives so early and departs so late.

She rises and finds an old-fashioned percolator and a container marked "freshly ground coffee" in a small shared common area of the guest-house. She takes the liberty of making it and perches on a high-top chair at the counter, awaiting its brew. Either the smell of the coffee or her clumsy clanking of mugs wakes other guests. An overweight, middle-aged white woman with overly plucked eyebrows, obviously also newly risen, joins her. Together they hold court waiting for the brewing cycle to end, instantly communing in a way known only to coffee drinkers and smokers.

"First time here?" the woman asks with a clipped, recognizable Jersey accent.

"Yes. Just arrived yesterday. Beautiful island. Such pleasant people." She smiles.

Ambrose is surprised when the woman rolls her eyes before asking, "Vacation?"

"Work trip. I'm a writer. You?"

"Visiting family. My husband is Puerto Rican, has an aunt here and cousins in San Juan." Then she adds, in a conspiratorial tone, "We prefer *not* to stay with them, ya know."

"I *do* know," replies Ambrose. "Family can be difficult."

"It's not so much family. It just this . . . uggg . . . this whole *culture*. I'm *not* staying in those tiny houses with chickens and goats running around. Don't get me wrong. We do what we can. We give to charity," she brags, as though philanthropy comes with the privilege of judgment.

"But these people just won't help themselves. Since you're writing about these people, lemme tell ya what they're really like," she says righteously. "All of these people are on welfare. All of them. They live it. They teach it to their kids as a way of life. They scam the system, and they don't even pay taxes. That's why they are so happy all the time. They get paid not to work. You and I support them. They refuse to work and still get paid."

The plucked woman folds her arms, smirking, waiting to be thanked for being the first to tell Ambrose how things really work on the island of Vieques.

Ambrose recalls the airport porter, the courteous waiters, the pleasant golf cart rental clerk, and Lucinda. In her short time here, she hasn't noticed a lack of workers or a lack of services.

Ambrose attempts a shrug-off. "My work isn't about welfare or politics."

"Oh, it's not politics," the woman asserts. "They're taking Democrat money just as much as they're taking Republican money. But it *is* the Democrats that keep them that way, ya know. They figure as long as they're givin' 'em free money, they'll keep voting 'em in."

Ambrose doesn't answer, glancing hopefully at the coffee. Her silence enables the woman, who assumes much by her failure to engage. Ambrose wonders if the woman knows her interpretation of the silence says more about herself than about Ambrose.

"It's true," she insists, doubling down. "The whole damn Puerto Rican government went bankrupt because of the corruption. And these people *still* keep getting their welfare checks. Not one person outside the US should get money from our government until all of our veterans are taken care of. Am I right?"

The irony would be laughable if this fat, overplucked woman weren't deadly serious in her fanatical insanity. Vieques is part of the United States, and its citizens have served its military. A third of this island is military. But the plucked Trump, as Ambrose has come to think of her, is in such an ideological stupor of hate and righteousness that she is far beyond the reach of the rational.

"It's the children I feel most bad for. Running around with no shoes, no doctors around, learning how to live off the system. They don't even teach them to speak American."

The woman grows more and more agitated by Ambrose's silence, desperate to find either agreement or argument. Ambrose gives her neither. Conversation is no longer possible or productive. Ambrose learned long ago that nothing is to be gained by engaging with someone so self-righteously committed in their own misguided certainty.

Ambrose holds her tongue but consciously shifts her angle, scans the room for possible weapons and nearby exits, and sizes up the woman. The Trumpette herself would pose no physical threat. Though twice Ambrose's size, the woman has already expended her limited energy on her indignant rant. Of more concern is Ambrose's absolute certainty the graciously appointed Caribbean-colored sanctuary of the room adjacent to her own houses a concealed weapon—a weapon this gun-loving Trumpster would feel justified in using.

"They can get to America. They don't even have to immigrate. There are jobs there. They just don't wanna work. What the fuck is wrong with them? Get off your ass and move and feed your fucking family. Fucking lazy. My husband grew up the same damn way these people did, and you don't see him begging for government handouts. He went to the mainland and got a good job. All these people could do the same. Our tax dollars pay for them to laze around on this tropical island. And if that doesn't piss you off, you must be a special kind of stupid."

The woman fumes, her unchallenged tirade morphing into a physical impediment—spewing spittle, pupils dilating, her puffed face comically distorting her pencil-thin eyebrows, cheeks and chest purpling with inflamed rosacea.

The burbling coffee maker mercifully stops, and Ambrose reaches out to fill her mug, ensuring she continues to face the woman as she moves. Marcus would be proud of the way she is protecting her back. Ambrose hopes her movement marks an end to the conversation.

"Enjoy your coffee. I hear it's locally grown, harvested, roasted, and even ground here," she says evenly and backs into her room, ignoring the woman's smug tsk-tsks and her last jab, which, in cowardice, lands after Ambrose closes her door.

"Fucking libtards."

CHAPTER 16

The road traversing the western portion of the island toward the World War II bunkers testifies to the hurricane's destruction. Large, once-lovely private villas dotting the mountain resemble disjoined sculptures of shattered beams and broken concrete. Smaller abodes fared better in the aftermath, lovingly made livable and tidy with patchworks of tin and plywood where needed. Only the wealthy could afford abandonment and waste.

The mountain foliage is less tropical than one might imagine—the greenery more akin to her native Appalachia than she expected, though thicker, shorter, more tangled with trees whose storied roots curve and twist, while those of the Appalachian Mountains follow a more upright path of growth.

The pines of the Appalachians grow straight and narrow, climbing ever higher, competing for sunlight, shedding toxic needles to kill what dares bloom in their shade. The vegetation of Vieques's forest is low and fat, its trees squatted together, sharing nourishment and sunlight in communal defense against the Atlantic's relentless, unceasing wind and salt and tides. The Appalachian forest enjoys the protected proximity of an enormous landmass, standing mighty and arrogant as though its dominance had been earned rather than an accident of geography. Vieques's mountain forest huddles alone and strong against a vast, unending, incessant ocean. Ambrose is fond of lone fighters.

The roadway is dotted with rusting sugarcane-harvesting equipment and set in a backdrop of deep, unnatural wounds in the mountainscape. Jagged and stark, these wounds are not the soft erosions of the rest of the island, exfoliated by saltwater air and vines. These are the mining cuts from the failed seawall.

She takes a left at a T in the road, driving toward the bunkers. The potholed road narrows to a trail with even more potholes. She approaches some low concave structures, huddled in groups of three, overgrown and viny. Stenciled military-style signs, weathered but still affixed, identify the bunkers numbered 314, 238, 203. Most of the thick doors are padlocked. She parks her golf cart in the shade and, finding one of the doors ajar, enters cautiously, turning on her phone's flashlight and recalling with some concern the unidentified animal sounds of this morning.

The domed exterior belies a spacious interior littered with a broken Coke machine, soggy mattresses, and bins from an abandoned recycling effort. Always on Vieques, abandoned. Other than some notably good graffiti, which she captures in pictures, the bunkers are unimpressive, neither imposing nor telling. Flat and dead.

She returns to her golf cart, happy to hear its purr, and follows the map toward the ruins of a sugar plantation. The trail narrows, creeping trees scraping the golf cart's roof, first occasionally, then relentlessly closing in. She is suddenly claustrophobic and acutely aware of her aloneness. She has encountered no one—no golf carts, no jeeps, no people, no island horses, not even an iguana—since she left the T in the road. She feels in danger of becoming yet another abandoned relic, flat and dead, on this twisted path.

She drives on, as fast as the encroaching greenery allows, hoping the pathway widens once more. Instead, the canopy becomes suffocatingly dense and entwined. The path is wide enough at its base for the golf cart, but the island trees join hands over it in a smothering game of London Bridge. Sunlight gasps through thick tree cover, giving way to green-black darkness.

Then it flashes, mutes, alters, the forest becoming more dense, younger, more aggressive. Once again, and even while wearing her prescription sunglasses, her vision blurs, then clears to the crisp and strong smell of roasting coffee beans and honey.

Tree limbs whip against her coal-black face as she flees, desperate and wild. Angry voices, clipped and abrasive, scream words she doesn't understand. Dogs, unleashed and chomping, yelp in chase. High mountain slopes and flat forests echo and trap sound, masking how many give chase or from which direction they come.

Driven by terror and confusion, she hasn't considered to where she might flee. The alien landscape, green and twisted and slithering, bewilders her. It is so different from her flat, pale savannah home many moons away and disorienting to senses dulled by the tedious monotony of an endless sea voyage. She is frail from the harsh journey and the sickness and atrophy it brought, from despair and loneliness, from the bland, colorless gruel devoid of nutrition. Her skin is withered and dusky, her hair sparse, and her ribs protruding. Her ankles are scabbed from chains.

The course burlap raiment draped around her before leaving the boat chafes her skin raw as she runs. She finds no path, no clearing, no comforting elder beyond the village of monolithic stone temples built one atop the other and evil iron beasts puffing fire.

The quicker she runs, the thicker becomes the relentless snarl of twisting trunks and creeping underbrush. Thin vined tentacles catch her arms, the undergrowth's current engulfs her feet, and she is pulled into the island's embrace.

As the dogs close in, the forest whispers there is no escape. Terror and a strong smell of roasting coffee.

Panicked, and confused by the visions that overwhelm her, Ambrose whips the golf cart into reverse and punches the gas pedal, following the pathway out of the tangled plantation, past the World Word II bunkers and the hurricane carnage until, relieved, she finds the T in the road. There her heart calms, soothed by the view—a coved bay, graced by an ocean so calm that in the distance pufferfish clouds vainly kiss their reflection.

Fuzzy and blinking, she is not sure what happened, even *if* it happened. "What the fuck was that?"

Maybe it was the rich forest overstory playing tricks on her travel-weary mind. Or maybe the island itself knows not the science and physics of the mainland. Now, though, having seen the terror of slavery, she understands in a visceral way why Vieques welcomed the military. Why they sacrificed their homes, cut their motherland, and gave their daughters and sons to the hope of America. Hope was enough.

CHAPTER 17

The Cortezes live in Isabel Segunda now, Vieques's version of a city. It feels foreign, with hints of South America. Friendly and low, Isabel Segunda is a confusing mix of urban and rural life—squat, flat houses painted turquoise and yellow and burnt orange, with caged windows plotted equidistant from one another on a measured grid. Rich plots, more like microfarms than gardens, flourish in backyards, with chickens and an occasional goat running free across potholed roads.

Houses are small on Vieques, not necessarily due to economics but because in the steady, long island days, life happens outside. Even midday, porches and side yards bustle. Old men plop on front porches, sink deep in rusty folding chairs, sipping from mason jars, puffing on fat cigars, and grunting low wisdoms to younger men who stand leaning against thin porch columns. The young men's time to sit has not yet come. Children roughhouse nearby while mothers hang laundry and gossip. Adolescent girls take carefully prepared grocery lists and a few dollars from their mother, traveling in groups to the *calmadito*, swaggering in importance from the responsibility. Teenage boys sauntering toward the beach watch the girls pass in admiration. The girls, feeling very grown up with the weight of familial trust, pretend to be above noticing.

In Isabel Segunda, unlike the rest of the island, people rely on cars big enough to absorb the shock of the massive potholes or scooters that can easily maneuver around them. Ambrose's struggle driving her rented golf cart through the streets of Isabel Segunda is being watched with curiosity and bemusement by all but the children, whose charm lies in their myopic self-absorption, which gives little notice to others' stupidity. Between being confused by the town's mish-mashed layout, avoiding potholes and stray chickens, and being unable to read the Spanish road signs, Ambrose is utterly perplexed.

One grizzled porch patriarch shouts out helpfully, "One way, *gringa*!" Embarrassed and disheveled, Ambrose guides the golf cart in an awkward U-turn and drives past the old man and his gaggle, who enjoy a good laugh at her expense.

She doesn't *find* the Cortezes' home. The family calls to her as she accidently drives by. They laugh as she awkwardly maneuvers the golf cart in a three-point turn that morphs into a five-point turn, beeping her incompetence each time she throws the gear into reverse.

"No wonder the plane was late," yells a young man from the porch in thickly accented English.

Finally pointed in the right direction, she parks in front of a faded turquoise square home and is greeted by a voluptuous, attractive woman who wipes her hand on her apron, presumably Lettie, Rick's cousin. Lettie opens the front gate and waves her in with a simple "Come, *mija*," as if Ambrose is already known and already knows.

But Ambrose does not know, and she wishes for the formality of introductions to untangle the web of relationships that create the intimate interlace of men and women and children that migrate in and out of the yard, creating the feel of a compound more than a city block. Do extended families live next to each other, or are some of the people laundering and shucking corn and sipping from mason jars neighbors?

"Hi, I'm Ambrose," she starts as a prompt.

The men lounging on the front porch laugh, one quipping, "*Sí*, who else would you be, *gringa*?"

An old man, perhaps the eldest, speaks to her, but Ambrose doesn't understand.

"*No habla español*," she says in shoddy Spanish. The brood of men breaks into laughter.

Another young man retorts, "She's got that right," and the oldest man slows his speech and tries once more.

"I *am* speaking English, *gringa*. I said, 'If the golf cart gives you trouble, you should stay away from the horses.'"

Ambrose blushes momentarily. Then the old man smiles one of those fighter's grins that tugs at her heart, and deep-set mischievous laugh lines curl toward his peppered hair, and she is charmed. She recognizes that the gauntlet has been laid, and the bell has rung.

"I stay away from asses, sir. As such, shall I join the ladies?"

The clan of porch sitters howls with laughter, as the quip is repeated in Spanish. The old man with the fighter's grin warms to affection, his eyes twinkle playfully, and he graces her a slow nod.

Lettie tsks, snaps a towel at the old man, and guides Ambrose to a seat among a coven of women shucking double-red corn around a large black trash can that resembles a cauldron. Lettie moves the container a bit closer to Ambrose and hands her a bag of corn still nestled in nature's silken cocoon. The woman next to Ambrose is regaling the cluster of women with an apparently captivating story in Spanish, and Ambrose's arrival does not create a pause in the story. Ambrose is given no more than a glance, as if she has always been there. Their indifference is oddly welcoming.

Reaching into the bag, she pulls out a piece of purplish-red corn and holds it momentarily in her hand. She looks around the circle, watching the women as they shuck corn so quickly Ambrose can't catch their hand movements. The storyteller next to her, without slowing her pace, takes the ear of corn from Ambrose's hand. Giving Ambrose a bemused glance, she turns the ear. She slows her movements, showing Ambrose how to pull the leaves down until the silk tassels show, tug firmly down to the base, throw the ripped cocoon in the waiting trash can and the fresh corn in a bin.

Ambrose shucks the next piece of corn. The task is more difficult than it looks, but once she shucks in rhythm, she finds hypnotic peace. The cadence of the hand motion melding into a living circle of femininity is powerful and nourishing, enabling Ambrose to grasp the island's contradictions in the rough husks and soft silks of its fruits. She is enchanted by the cosmic shades of purples and blues and reds that emerge with each tug and the lulling sounds of Spanish that flow over her as soothing vocals. In a daze, Ambrose lets go of all the complexities of language, all of the sounds intertwining to create a sensory meridian that is tribally connective. The gentle cacophony is ancestral and earthen and essential. In this moment, shucking corn is the most satisfying and important work she has ever done. There is no poverty here.

She also understands her conventional interview will not happen—no measured questions, no direct answers, no clever follow-ups. In a place where no introductions are needed, she doubts questions are allowed.

The language barrier is too great. She is surprised how few among the coven know English, even among the children. This is, after all, still America, yet English is not taught in the schools. She mentally puts learning Spanish on her bucket list.

For a while, she tries to follow the conversation, putting bits together. The effort proves exhausting and unproductive. Instead, she decides to think of the situation as a writing prompt, one of those literary games Will is so fond of.

"For this one," she can almost hear him saying, "you can't understand anything the characters are saying. Use context, observe reactions and relationships, and use your senses to *feel* the conversation."

He would listen, feigning rapture, not with an eye to improving her writing but to chart the recesses of her mind, building a psychological map for future manipulation.

She doesn't need to understand the language to comprehend the connections between these women. She feels the tones, sees the body language, and detects the good-natured bantering.

Eventually, after much bustling, Lettie settles in next to Ambrose.

"How do you like Vieques?" Lettie asks.

"I like it very much, thank you. Everything here is so beautiful, and you are very kind to welcome me," Ambrose replies. "Did Rick tell you I am writing a book about your family?"

"*Sí*, a book." Lettie nods, polite but unimpressed.

"I hope to get some background about what it was like to grow up here in the 1940s, especially the community's relations with the military."

"We could shuck all the island's corn and still be answering that question, *mija*," Lettie smirks.

"Yeah, I suppose so." She glances over to the brood of men on the porch. "Did any of these men serve in the military?"

Lettie lowers her gaze and says quietly, "Do not ask the men about the military, *mija*." Ambrose takes a breath. Lettie pauses, glances back at the men, and lowers her voice. "They are good men. There were some good men in the military too. At least the ones who were stationed here. They lived alongside us. Visited our homes. Ate and drank with us. They paid our women to do laundry and clean. Men like Rick's dad. Good men. But there were no jobs for island men, and it made them feel less like men to see other men with jobs court their women, pay their mothers, even if they did it honorably."

She sighs. "And then there were the military visitors—large groups of men who came to the island to train for a few weeks. Thousands of them. Sometimes there were more visitors than Viequenses on this island. And the military would give them leave. Thousands of men in our towns meant for hundreds—wanting food and liquor and more. They stole; they destroyed. We learned to hide and lock the doors when they came. But still . . . bad things happened when they were here. When those bad things happened, it was almost worse for the men than the girls. Because the men couldn't protect their wives and their daughters, and there is nothing worse for men of honor. I think it lives with the men who feel they failed even more than the women who paid the price."

"The military let that happen?"

"They would give money when stores were destroyed. But the next time the visitor soldiers came, the destruction would happen again. And some things cannot be paid for in dollars." She pauses, concentrating on tugging the husks. "No, *mami*, do not ask the men about the military."

Ambrose nods knowingly and chooses her next question with care. "Does anyone recall visiting the doctors on the base in the 1940s?"

Lettie accepts that this is a question that can be asked. She raises her voice to the coven, triggering an animated conversation authored by several older women. Their voices rise and fall, waving with good-natured arguing punctuated by laughter, heads sometimes nodding, sometimes shaking, pointing ears of corn to the east, occasional interjections of playful bantering from younger women. Ambrose watches the process of history being written as a negotiation of shared memory.

Lettie acts as interpreter. "*Sí*, they went to doctors on that base," she says, pointing east. "And now we don't even have that. The hospital wasn't rebuilt after the hurricane, so now we are worse off than we were in the 1940s."

The conversation continues, growing more animated.

"They say the military should reopen the clinic on the base. The building still stands, though it is in ruins—Gate G. It could be rebuilt. Or they could open one on the new base."

Laughter interrupts, and Lettie chuckles to herself. "They say that with all the military dumped on this island, Viequenses are probably immune to everything. Don't even need vaccines!"

"How do they know the clinic is still there? Isn't that in the red zone, where there are unexploded ordnance and chemical dumps? And what do they mean, 'new military base'? I thought the military withdrew."

Lettie doesn't need to consult the group this time. "There's still a military base on the east of the island. They say it's to oversee what remains. And *sí*, MEDCOM still stands. It's in the red zone, but we know which areas are safe and which are not. Gate G does not have unexploded ordnance. That area wasn't used for bombs. It was used for the clinic."

"People still go up there?"

"*Sí*, young couples sneak in when they want to be alone," she whispers conspiratorially.

"How do ya know it's safe?"

"Memory and horse shit."

Ambrose is taken aback for a moment, before Lettie laughs good-naturedly. "The horses know. Not one horse has ever been blown up. If you follow the trail of horse shit, you follow a clear path."

———

After much shucking and some cool island tea, Ambrose pulls herself reluctantly from the enchanted circle. She cedes a winning nod to the old man with the fighter's grin as he teases an offer of a helmet as she climbs back into the golf cart. She opens her cartoonish map of the island, causing a fresh eruption of laughter from the gaggle of men on the porch. "There are only four roads, *gringa*," the old man calls out. "Where to?"

"The cemetery," she shouts back.

He points north. She waves again, and one of the men quips, "Someone better warn the dead she's coming!"

Ambrose laughs with them and waves as she pulls the cart into the road, barely missing a chicken.

CHAPTER 18

It is a crowded, unexpectedly lively cemetery set high on a rocky northern mount overlooking the azure ocean, with Puerto Rico in the background only a few miles in the distance. It reminds her of New Orleans and vampires and voodoo. Low iron gates protect aged sarcophagi. Encased coffins are laid above ground, rather than buried below, giving a sense that the dead are close, still just a breath away. The weathering of the iron and cement lends a rich marbled patina in the dappled sunshine. Large, simple crosses don almost every tomb sloping the overlook, like hundreds of children standing with their arms open in an eternal welcoming of the sun. She has the vague feeling that when Jesus returns, those children will finally be released to frolic on the beach, the ocean's briny waters soothing their blanched arms.

Adding to the sense of life in this bedroom of the dead is a quirky mix of foliage. Wild weeds erupt from the earth in defiance of the cement burden laid upon it. Mango trees on grassy knolls bear heavy, ripened fruit, with island horses feeding lazily on the juicy bounty below.

Here, burial plots and sarcophagi nurture life. Alongside burial chambers are tended gardens of hostas and herbs, with ornate cement planters built atop the tombs or intricate garden baskets attached to gates. Ambrose happens upon several families weeding the plots, laughing and scolding children. Should she happen upon a spirit or a ghost, she isn't sure she could distinguish them from the living.

Nowhere to be seen are the cut flowers or wreaths popular in Philly— offerings laid upon the dead, dying. No, this cemetery is not built for remorse or sadness or loneliness. The dead here, and the dead's home, are very much a vivid part of daily family life. The parsley on your fish might well have been pulled from beside Aunt Leona's grave.

Accompanying the blooming flowers and herbs are offerings, some laid on small, low tables with richly colored cloths. Staggered rows of dripped wax candles burned to wick crowd each other, creating Rasta patterns at the feet of the fallen. Bundled dried herbs, small bright bags, chalices half full of black coffee, and an occasional nip of Crab Island Rum sit in homage to small santos and sainted cards. Several she recognizes as the black Virgin Mary she saw at Philomena's kitchen and in her guesthouse room, with a snake and an infant curled in her lap. Ambrose snaps pictures, enchanted by the patterns and textures of this vivacious cemetery, marveling at the endless contradictions on this island.

She wanders through this graveyard that feels more like a garden, loosely following the directions Lettie gave her. Mirroring her arrival at the Cortezes' earlier that day, she doesn't really *find* the family's garden plot; it finds her. Admiring the rich canopy over her, she trips on an errant tree root and finds herself squarely facing a phalanx of dead Cortezes. Steadying herself, she ventures off the main path to walk among the Cortezes' ancestors. She wonders briefly how an island so poor can afford the elaborate, ornate stone and iron work.

Since the beginning of mankind, humans have held as sacred the care of their dead, burying with them weapons and food and precious objects. The practice of burying valuable objects in resource-deprived communities, of spending precious energy and time on caring for and honoring the dead when energy and time are elemental to survival, simply doesn't make sense to her. Yet humans, and only humans, have held the practice since time immemorial. The belief systems and specific practices and rites change through time and culture and geography, but across humanity, mankind invests illogically in death.

Her musing comes to an end when she notices the mismatched carvings at the edge of the Cortezes' garden, recognizing the names. Inscribed formally in measured cursive on a high sarcophagus with a small American flag leaning in an iron vase is *"Juan Cortez, dio su vida al servicio de su país, 7/4/1925–11/22/1943."* Chiseled with an endearing imperfection that possesses all the passion of hearts carved eternal in an old oak tree is a second name: *"Sweet Javier. Volver a Casa."* She uses her phone to translate.

The formal writing reads, "who gave his life in service of his country"; the oak tree etching, "Come Home."

An anomaly in the patterns of the grave gardens just east of the Cortezes catches her eye, and she moves closer to explore. More traditional headstones erupt on this plot, looking squat and plain and out of place among the large, ornate sarcophagi. It is dedicated to a family named Speak, engraved with no Christian names, just spelled in English, "Mother" and "Father," followed by "love~forgiveness~compassion." Speak, Mother, Father. Ambrose knows that is the message Philomena said Spirit has left her. If Spirit meant to land a sucker punch, it worked. She reels for a moment from emotion, then gives herself grace to put her reaction aside for the moment, knowing she is not capable of processing her feelings productively after a long and emotional day.

Turning away from a message she doesn't want to see, she notices an unpaved, informal pathway leading down the mountain. She is called to follow the path through thick brush with high bridging tree branches for some time, until it opens up to a cliff overlooking the ocean before curving toward the village. She pauses at the cliff, hypnotized by the ripple of the distant waves shimmering in the late afternoon sun, rhythmic and lulling, before her vision blurs and crisps and the smell of roasting coffee and honey returns.

A young family breaks as the soldiers perform a saluted retreat from the casket, and the priest in his violet vestments leads the final signum crucis, *to the north, the south, the east, the west, committing a soul in the name of the Father, the Son, and the Holy Spirit.*

The eldest young hugs a thick, folded triangle—a silken blue standard stitched with forty-eight crisp white stars. There is no star for Puerto Rico, no star for Vieques. The sacrifice of the sons of Puerto Rico may earn the honor of a military funeral but not the badge of a star stitched upon its nation's standard. The eldest young hugs the flag to her chest just the same, because she needs to hug something. She snuggles into the awaiting arms of the handsome American soldier beside her for a moment, and he kisses her tenderly on her forehead. She turns to her sister, speaking in the English she is learning from her beau.

"Philomena, go down the back path quickly. The parade will begin soon. Start the coffee; put out the food; light the candles. We will have many guests to feed." Philomena obediently turns toward the path before her sister pauses. "Wait. Take this with you, mija.*" She pulls from her neck a portrait charm with an onyx woman draped in green and gold with a child and a snake in her lap. She drapes the charm and the long pendulum chain on which it rests around Philomena's neck. "Santa Marta protect you." She crosses to the east, the west, the south, and the north, the reverse of the cross just performed by the priest. The girls see no contradiction.*

Philomena follows the path quickly to beat the crowd of mourners home. Her head is down, tears of anguish still coming in waves. Her hands grasp the medallion for comfort. Voices carry as the brushed path bends and opens, cliffing to the ocean. Men's voices. American men's voices.

"Makes me sick to hand an American flag to some spic bitch."

"Dishonoring our flag. Fucking waste of money and time us even being here."

"Why they even let them in to the military? I don't want no dirty spic in my foxhole."

"What else are they gonna do with these fucking people? They gotta gid rid of 'em somehow."

She recognizes two Americans clad in crisp battle dress who have just borne the weight of her brother's casket and sent him to rest with a solemn salute. They sit at the edge of the cliff, facing away from her, feet dangling over the rocky ocean below, each with one camouflage sleeve rolled past their elbows. She is close enough to the first to see a deep red birthmark that splatters the back of his neck, extending behind his ear and into his buzzed ginger hairline. He habitually scratches it.

The Birthmarked One secures a black rubber tourniquet around his bicep with his teeth. She hears the scraping flick of a lighter. She smells something burnt and bitter and tinny and watches as he holds a syringe, tapping at it before easing the sharp tip into his arm.

"They should just let us shoot 'em. Be better than all these drawn-out expensive solutions they got for 'em. Hell, at least Hitler gets some work outta the Jews."

"But how ya gonna do that to US citizens?"

"Ya make 'em not US citizens. They're not real citizens. Never will be."

The Birthmarked One inhales deeply and sighs as the drug jolts his body alive. He bolts to his feet and walks the sharp edges of the cliff's rocks unsteady, jittery, incomprehensibly fearless and certain.

"Could make a whole war game of it. Give 'em the whole island, and me, one machine gun and some ammo. Maybe a shank so I can kill some of 'em slow." He turns toward the cliff, beats his chest, and screams to the ocean, "I'd kill 'em all in a week!"

Philomena has learned some English alongside her sister, but the soldiers are talking so fast. She understands the bitter tone of hatred enough to attempt a silent, slow retreat.

She fails. As the Birthmarked One turns from his rant, he catches her backing away along the trail. "What are you looking at, spic bitch?"

She freezes.

He saunters down from the rocks toward her. "Catch ya checking out the white dick, hun?" He grabs his crotch. "Gotcha curious? Why don't you ask your sister? She's fucking one of our boys. Makes me fuckin' sick."

The other soldier, still sitting on the rocks, turns, nervously biting his nails. "For Christ's sake, leave Robby alone, will ya? He's been on this island for years. What else he gonna fuck? Goats?"

The Birthmarked One nears her, and still she is frozen. He stands over her, looking down, a foot taller than her. He smells of mechanic grease and lye. His pupils are dilated, and the whites of his eyes are bloodshot. His skin is blotched red, the perspiration on his upper lip mixing with snot. His mouth kneads as if he were chewing chaw or gum, but he is not. In each chud, he expels a bitter breath that makes her nauseous.

"I'd rather fuck a goat. But I don't see one around."

She turns her head slightly to escape the veil of his breath and listens for someone coming down the path.

"Oh, you ain't going anywhere. And ain't no one gonna come. Today is your lucky day, spic bitch. We're gonna satisfy your curiosity."

He effortlessly grabs her small frame and pulls her hair, forcing her to look at him. He considers her for a moment before spewing, "Nah." He says slowly, "I don't even wanna look at you."

He flips her over and takes her to the ground. He holds her face to the earth and pulls her pelvis toward him. She kicks back, pushes up, squirms to no avail. In the struggle, he rips her underwear from her body.

The second soldier comes to stand in front of her. She sees scuffs on his army-issued boots, which looked shiny just moments ago when he offered her brother's final salute. Now she can see marks blotted with black pen and frayed shoelaces knotted through the eyelets to keep them together. A spider crawls over the boot as she watches. It pauses at an eyelet knot, scurries around the obstacle toward the toe, and jumps a dismount unnoticed by the wearer.

Beyond the boots and the spider, the rocks merge browns and reds and grays in hues so muted by nature's wear it is hard to distinguish one color from another. And beyond the rocks, the sparkles skiffing on the distance ocean bring her a dazed comfort.

"They're some kinda Catholic voodoo, ya know. They'll give you head and let ya fuck 'em in the ass," says the spider-boot soldier. He unbuckles

his pants, pulls out his cock before her, grabs her hair, and pulls back her head. Her eyes squish shut.

"Open your eyes, spic bitch. You're gonna look at me the whole time."

She fails to obey. He tightens his grip on her hair and smacks her. Her eyes open reactively. "There we go. That's better."

The pendant her sister gave her hangs from her neck, swinging back and forth beneath her. She snuggles it in her hand, closes her eyes, and invokes silently, "Santa Marta la Dominadora, protect me."

"Whatcha got there?"

He grabs at her hand, but she won't let go. He tugs hard, breaking the chain. The pendant scuffles across the ground. He picks it up and looks at it. "What the fuck is this? A black Virgin Mary?" he spits in disgust. "Virgin Mary ain't black, you stupid spic. Sick fucks, defiling the mother of our Lord. Y'all goin' straight to hell."

The Birthmarked One tears her from behind. She screams. His large, pasty hand covers her mouth. And she drowns in pain, engulfed in her own screams.

Then she is free. She falls to her side and shrivels into a protective ball. As her own screams fade, the screams of the soldiers come into focus.

"What the fuck? Where did these fuckers come from?"

Steadying herself on one elbow, she turns around to see the Birthmarked One still kneeling, an enormous boa constrictor wrapped around his legs, preventing his rise. His dick stills hangs, now shriveled and flaccid. He strikes at the boa with his fists uselessly. The enormous snake slowly, methodically embraces him. The soldier's struggle only serves to further seal his fate. He topples to his side with a lumbered, ungainly thump.

The spider-boot soldier is frantically circling backward as another large boa approaches him, dispassionate and lazy. Philomena hears rustling in the trees in stereo as two more boas from either side of the clearing drop from trees and circle the soldier, creating a slow, stifling noose around him. He backs farther and farther, until he edges the cliff. In contrast to the unhurried, measured corralling, when the lead boa strikes, it is with startling velocity. The strike lands with fangs deep into the soldier's thigh meat, simultaneously coiling round his legs. Caught off balance, the soldier extends his arms and steels his core for balance. He looks for a moment like Jesus on the cross. It is a hopeless cause. He cannot balance under the relentless, swaying strength of the boa. They teeter for an infinite, teasing moment on the edge of life and death, long enough for him to wonder if the jagged rocks or waterlogged lungs will kill him first, before the tangle of man and boa topples over the edge.

A deep, fading scream is followed by a distant thud. In the ensuing silence is the sound of soft, rhythmic waves breaking, undisturbed by life or death. Philomena bear-crawls, panicked, to the cliff's edge, scanning the rocked shoreline, trying to discern a figure human among nature's worn hues. The soldier and the boa have been swallowed in the camouflaged blues of the Atlantic. The ocean sparkles, its undulating rhythm lulling her, whispering that it will all be over soon. There is no more danger here. Trusting the ocean, she turns back toward what is no longer a danger.

The two boas that had cornered the now-fallen soldier cross, one over the other, in a slow, slithering, shifting crucifix before disappearing back to the island's tangled, flourishing underbrush.

The Birthmarked One is now completely engulfed by the thick-muscled serpent, his arms pinned awkward and unnatural, still cocooned and powerless on his side. And the great boa comes to face him, eye to eye, its large triangled head, big and thick as a Rottweiler's, swaying back and forth, pondering. The serpent gives one last smothering embrace, and the Birthmarked One shits and pisses himself. The boa opens its mouth in a perverse, teasing smile and flicks its tongue. The Birthmarked One feels moist sandpaper on his face, his eyes wide and red, his mouth open in a truncated scream. He can't draw enough air into his lungs to match the spirit of the scream with sound. With lightning speed, the boa lashes and snags its fangs across the Birthmarked One's cheek, leaving twin trails of blood. Then, as quick as it came, the sinuous beast uncoils and disappears into the brush.

The Birthmarked One convulses in a desperate contradiction of sucking air and coughing. He writhes, soiled, puked bile dripping from his chin, his *shoulder hanging out of its socket. When his breathing calms into the shallows of pain, his gaze finds her. They hold each other's eyes in a long bewildering moment of swapped indignity before he inhales and rasps, "Help."*

Philomena arises slow and methodical as if the boas had shed their spirit to her. She looms over the Birthmarked One, whose desperate eyes register relief. She stands hovering for a long moment. When she bends down, he recoils into a defensive ball, whimpering from pain. She ignores him, retrieving her sister's pendant, lying among his puke. Once more the pendant finds a cradle in her palm, and she whispers, "Gracias, Santa Marta la Dominadora." She does not clean the bile from the pendant, knowing the body fluid of an enemy carries powerful mojo and trusting Santa Marta designed it to have it.

Still standing over the Birthmarked One, she secures the clasp to a new link on the chain, pulling the pendant closer against her throat. She feels his bile feed the fleshly vitality of her neck, just above the notch in her collarbone. When it is secured, she rises to her full height and finally turns her attention to the writhing mess at her feet, while he continues a depthless chant for help. She considers him a moment and answers him flat and cold.

"No hablo inglés."

She retrieves her torn underwear and shoves it in her pocket before turning her back to him without fear.

"You can't leave me here like this," he screams to her retreating back. "God damn you!"

"Sí, he will." She nods without turning back. She understands a life has been taken at her bidding and payment will come due.

She turns to face that curse and make the coffee for the guests of her brother's funeral, leaving the Birthmarked One steeped in the stench of his own shit and the odd smell of coffee and honey.

Philomena's energy lingers as the ocean's skiffing sparkles come back into focus. Ambrose is heartsick and awakened, more confident in the visions each time they come. As she turns to leave this sad and beautiful place, she is certain she catches the golden-brown shimmer of a boa in the underbrush.

CHAPTER 19

After seeking the nourishment of fish and plantains and grounding herself back in the twenty-first century, she follows the *Where's Waldo* map to Playa Negra. A long, horse-dotted path leads to a beach of volcanic sand—obsidian black and magnetic, heavy and fine, velvety and soft. It is the polar opposite of the irritating and grainy sands of the mainland's east coast. Mesmerized, she watches the tide incessantly lap the ocean sands, bleached from churning, upon the velvet-black shore. The weight and magnetic properties of the native sand strongly bond its grains. Unable to penetrate the volcanic grit, the ocean's sand slides back to the sea, creating an undulating pattern of black and tan upon the shoreline like marbled peanut butter fudge. She takes a few pictures and instinctively flips open Snap to send them to Marcus before remembering she has blocked him.

Travel is supposed to open your mind, help you forget, she thought, not be a reminder of what was left behind. She wants to share with Marcus all the fascinations of this paradoxical paradise, the surprising sweetness of fried plantains, the deranged mind of the plucked Trump, and the frisky island horses running from angry owners. How might being with him in the bright bed of the guesthouse, so airy and light, compare to having him the in the dark, heavy Philly fight club?

The one thing she will never share with him is the visions; those are beyond the reach of words, but his strength would ease her, ground her. Even here, a thousand miles away, he is close—his voice, his scent, the curve of his shoulders over her—a little like the visions but shallow and ever present.

It isn't like that for him. People are transient in his world. Women rotate through his life like a carousel, always a few in play, others in check, still others in reserve. He is carefree and blithe and open, easily replacing people. She is serious and focused and closed, connecting with difficulty. Rare. She aches from loving him alone, and she aches from him loving everyone. To him, she could be anyone. To her, no one can be him. Or at least that's what she thinks. She never gave him a chance to answer. Maybe she created distance where she didn't want it, and that makes her heart ache even more. She settles with the pain for a long time, cradled in warm and giving sand that feels like both strength and forgiveness, before reaching for her phone.

hi

She waits a few minutes, digging a bit farther into the sand as her body begins to respond to the thought of him. Snap shows he read the message but has given no answer. She messages again.

Add me back and i will tell you how my trip is going

No answer.

can we talk

Finally he answers.

u talk all this shit about trust, but u can't even be trusted to hold a fucking conversation

u run & hide. its fucking cowardice. im not trying to fix bonds I didn't fucking break. u wanted me gone, im gone

He is right. Every word. She snuggles a bit deeper into the warm, forgiving sand. She lies there for a long time, sad and confused. His stinging rejection itself is hard to absorb but only part of the sadness.

She has rejected others the way she is now being rejected, almost habitually. She didn't know it felt like this—belittled and disposed of. In her self-righteous instinct to guard, she hadn't thought of how her actions made others feel. She remembers the graveyard message.

Opening her phone's contacts, she finds Mom and Dad. She has never deleted them. She doesn't hate them, though she has come to accept her mother hates her. Her mother has never particularly liked Ambrose. Ambrose is brash and difficult, and many people don't like her. But that's not why her mother hates her. Ambrose's mother hates her because Ambrose told, because she continues to tell. In her mother's eyes, the stigma Ambrose brought to the family by talking about what happened was far more horrifying than what actually happened. Her mother expects one to deal with such things personally—bear whatever burden is placed upon you in silence and dignity; smile pretty and, for the sake of the family, don't let your mascara run. Her mother needs to be the patient, sainted matriarch who bears the burden of the dependent, unstable, difficult child that is Ambrose. When Ambrose grew independent and owned what happened, publicly, she embarrassed her mother. To her mother, Ambrose is still unstable and ill, an even greater burden to the family. It doesn't escape Ambrose that her mother never doubted it happened. She never showed concern that Ambrose had been traumatized for much of her childhood, only that she had brought the truth to light. Ambrose wonders how long her mother knew, or suspected, and did nothing, willingly sacrificing her child for a golden crucifix and membership at the country club. Ambrose's mother needs to live in a reality where Ambrose is broken. Ambrose needs to live in a reality where society is broken. It is a deep-seated psychological stalemate.

Often, Ambrose hears or reads a well-intentioned explanation of how predators groom their victims. A predator lies, threatens parents will be angry with the victim, convincing their prey that their family will send them away, won't love them anymore. The saddest part is the predator isn't lying.

She closes her phone without dialing the number. She is willing to self-reflect, to take responsibility for her actions, to rethink her response to many things. But she is not willing to give up her hard-fought stability to join her mother's reality that requires she be broken. Graveyard message or not.

CHAPTER 20

The following day she turns her golf cart east. This time, the roads are wide and clear. A formal brown sign bordered in brick announces she is entering a US Fish and Wildlife Service National Wildlife Refuge. The road edges the base of the eastern mountain, with occasional trails veering right toward public beaches. She follows the access road for several miles—a lifetime on this island and in this golf cart—before she happens upon it. The entrance is not hidden. She pulls up to an innocuous yellow car gate, padlocked and marked "Gate G." A three-paneled sign, one of many along the road, defines the UXO warning area, instructing pedestrians to "Recognize, Retreat, and Report" if they happen upon unexploded ordnance and warning them to stay clear of red zones. No mention is made of chemicals or biological hazards, lost nuclear weapons, or "substances of unknown origin."

Regretfully leaving the golf cart behind, she jumps over the gate and hugs the north side of the trail, leaning into the shade from the forest trees and following horse shit. She wonders if following piles of horse shit on a toxic island on a trip she can't afford qualifies as rock bottom.

The hike is several steep miles, and for once, she is grateful her training included three dreaded runs per week. A few times she startles from wild/not-wild horses, but the trail is otherwise devoid of movement from the brown underbrush and low, leafy trees.

Cleared of vegetation and flattened amid the brown brush, the compound emerges—a paved pathway that could pass as a long, wide driveway had it not displayed the faint markings of an airstrip. She instinctively surveys the edges of the clearing the way a thief cases a joint. The area is quiet and deserted. Clocking her location on her phone, she begins taking pictures. She captures close-ups of the 09 at the far end of the runway, and of the tarmac, pimpled with opportunistic trees in some areas and bearded with vines in others.

A rickety domed hanger, not much bigger than a garage, crouches on the north end of the landing strip, an antique gas pump to its side, with two large sheds peeking from its rear.

At the far end of the landing strip, two low, gray cinder block buildings are connected by a shared entry. They are constructed more like the squat squares of the native homes rather than the convex bunkers on the eastern end of the island, with silos towering behind them.

The entire complex is untended and wild, with undergrowth and overgrowth and side growth, except for large bald patches surrounding the sheds to the rear of the hangar, giving the appearance of an ingrown hair in a beard.

Walking the tarmac has an eerie, postapocalyptic feel, still and unnerving. The setting contrasts oddly with the lush, vivacious cemetery she visited the day before. The tin hangar is rusty, its sliding doors dangling from their hinges. She ducks under one and takes off her prescription sunglasses, giving her eyes a moment to adjust to both the darkness and the blurriness. When they do, the shadow of a small ancient biplane comes into focus. She smiles in spite of herself. With a clown nose, a large mustache of a propeller, an industrial engine, and two open cockpits, the plane reminds her of Snoopy's Sopwith Camel. Adjusting the flash settings on her phone, she snaps more photos.

She captures the quaint "Fire Extinguisher" sign posted just below the cockpit and the ARMY decal and stars gracing the bottom of the plane. The insignia toward the tail resembles two faded upside-down commas crisscrossed at the stems and encased in a blue hexagon.

Turning away from the plane, she wanders about the hangar. Rusted tools and parts hang in disarray. A weathered flag hangs above the door. As with the plane's insignia, the flag is blue and gold. The banner sports a medieval dragon, a tree stump, and written words she assumes are Latin. She documents them in photos. Leaving through the back door, she slips on her sunglasses and steps into the baldness encompassing the large sheds to the rear of the hangar.

The sheds sit atop sagging pallets. Large, peeling warning labels proclaim in faded yellow and black, "Caution: Fertilizer Storage," and in red diamond icons, exclamation points, a fire, and a skull and crossbones. Hoses from the shed enter the hangar through designed openings. A large, oxidized trailer bin with a mechanized chute sits to the shed's rear. Ambrose documents with photos before following the tarmac toward the low cylindric buildings.

The island has begun to reclaim the buildings. Small trees and thick vines boa walls and windows, tugging them toward earth. She needn't open the thick bunker-style door—it stands ajar. She enters a spacious, bare reception area with a utilitarian desk and massive filing cabinets covered in dust. She can almost see a coiffed young cadet in a crisp pencil military skirt and 1950s red lipstick greeting her with a smile and an offer of coffee.

Ambrose checks her phone's battery and switches on its flashlight. She opens the desk's drawers and flips through its meager contents. She snaps a photo of a clipboard marked "Property of the US Army: CWS" and sporting the same comma-crossed emblem found on the plane. The filing cabinets are unlocked and empty. It couldn't be that easy, she thinks.

Massive twin doors face each other from opposite sides of the reception area. She tests the door to the southern wing first. It is heavy and cumbersome but opens easily to a small classic doctor's waiting room. The room is dark, with only a small, high window filtering daylight through decades of scum. The faded scrub-green walls match the cracked checkerboard floor tiles. Classic wooden school chairs are strewn in disarray. The sliding window to the receptionist area is still attached. Ambrose peeks into the receptionist area and tests the drawers and filing cabinets, which she finds, once more, unlocked and empty.

Following the hall, she discovers twin exam rooms. She enters one. It has a classic exam table as its centerpiece—a flat, uncomfortable table with a simple metal skeleton oxidizing through filthy white paint. Worn leather straps flop flaccid at its side, and light from her camera catches glints of thick metal buckles dangling at their ends, flashing their true menace. A chipped enamel bedpan stands ready below the table. Shelved apothecary cabinets, fronted in thick glass, still hold metal trays with tourniquets, long metal syringes, and chunky glass bottles with peeling typed labels. Several painted white iron stands hold large bowls with yellowing hand towels and rubber tubes draped over them just so, as if Nurse Ratched from *One Flew Over the Cuckoo's Nest* would be back in just a moment.

Ambrose notes the decrepit room has a creepy horror-movie vibe, but nothing seems odd or incriminating or out of place for a 1940s exam room—at least to her untrained eyes. Except that according to military records, this clinic does not exist.

Ambrose's picture-snapping adds to the horror-movie feel, giving an eerie cinematic flashing like a nickelodeon movie.

Making her way out of the exam room, she follows the hall to its end at a door marked "Staff Only." The smell of rotten mulch and decomposed animal corpses reborn as larvae nests overtakes her before the door is even fully open. The lab she finds behind the door matches the smell—it is Frankensteinian. High-topped high school chemistry tables are strewn with microscopes, moldy petri dishes, and stained vials. Large glass jugs hover over ancient Bunsen burners tubing up and out and spiraling into metal flasks. Circling the dank room, she takes photos of shelves with jars with typewritten labels that fill an entire wall. Rusting metal pipes enter the building from the northern wall and connect to large vats. Along that wall is a series of small, high barred windows. She jumps to catch the bars and, using her feet for leverage, climbs up to follow the pipes outside. Once she has struggled her way up, she realizes the flaw in her plan—having taken off her prescription sunglasses, she can't see. She laments a moment the effort it took to have achieved this perch, then sighs, jumps down, flips her glasses from her head to her nose, and repeats the ugly climbing pull-up to reclaim her vantage point. She should've heeded Marcus's long-tenured advice to work on pull-ups. Pull-ups are a weak point for her, and it's all she can do to hold the bars for fifteen seconds.

She sees enough to add to her confusion. The pipes exit the lab into a large, peeling vat in a courtyard behind the building. Large stickers on the vat are too far away and too faded to read, even with her glasses on, but clearly convey the vat's contents warrant warning. Pipes octopus from the vat, forming a neat network entering into the other wing of building. Windows, high and small like this one, line the northern wing, creating an ordered pattern of pipes and windows and concrete.

Behind the building a heavy tarp, or perhaps several overlapped, covers a mound about half the building's height and half its length. The mound is enclosed by a modern gate posted with warning signs. Feeling a bit like she is being subjected to a vision test, Ambrose finds she can read the first two lines of the warning posts: "Danger: Asbestos"; "Caution: Asbestos Hazard." Kev's mesothelioma theory is suddenly quite valid, if they can figure out how the progression of a disease taking decades to develop can be condensed into months.

Behind the mound and shadowed by tall silos are industrial-sized farming mixers akin to those settled near the hangar. The ground beneath the mixers is littered with . . . corn? She loses her grip and jumps once more to the lab floor.

Corn? Really? What if she is wrong? What if the military's intent really was to give medical care and food aid in a gesture of good will?

The methodology just seems odd by today's standards. What if she has spent all this time and money, and burnt bridges at home, chasing ghosts?

Glasses still on, she catches an odd sight on the western wall. She flips her glasses to rest on her head, lets her eyes adjust to the darkness once more, and warily moves closer. Lining the shelves of the wall are not medical vials and flasks but dozens and dozens of large terrariums. Some broken, some now home to spiderwebs and birds' nests. Enough are intact to find the source of the rotted smell—ancient mulch, a few shallow dishes, and the skeletons of clipped heat lamps. This equipment was not meant for humans.

She shudders a moment, wondering what could still be lurking or slithering in the corners. She snaps photos quickly, eager to leave, when she hears the heavy humming of an approaching vehicle.

She freezes dead still for a moment to judge the direction of its approach—it's coming in from the tarmac. She flees the lab, running down the hall and into the southern-facing exam room. She jumps and catches the bars of the high, small window and pulls/climbs herself up to peek out. A black, unmarked military-style transport parks in front of the building. A tall, thin woman in flawless dress greens emerges from the passenger seat as a dozen armed, gas-masked soldiers spill from its back. The soldiers follow the Tall Woman's beacons like bees around the queen, moving before her with guns drawn as they approach the building, while others disperse out of view.

"Holy shit," Ambrose whispers, jumping down from her perch and realizing the reception room is the only way in or out. Even if there were another exit, where would she run? Thinking quickly, she taps her phone to Snap.

marcus i need you.

Then, she group Snaps to both Kev and Marcus.

screenshot these! military about to find me

She makes herself small in the corner of the room next to the door, hoping to hide the phone's light. She hears the muffled call of soldiers beginning to sweep the building. She closes her eyes in a moment of gratitude as they move away, sweeping the northern wing first, buying her a few precious moments. Her blood rises, her heart pounds, her core churns—it's like the moment right before the bell rings. She breathes and focuses, quickly Snapping as many pictures as she can.

The soldiers' voices are becoming more clear, closer. Marcus has seen the Snaps, and notifications pop up one after another.

2nddegreeMarcus has screenshotted your Snap. Tears of relief well. She types, *thx*

2nddegreeMarcus: *i told you i am not your enemy*

KickboxAmbrose: *enemies are easy—they can't hurt me—u can*

Then she adds, *so much i want to say*

2nddegreeMarcus: *well that's new*

KickboxAmbrose: *i have to delete snap now*

2nddegreeMarcus: *u r a us citizen u have rights don't tell them anything. this is the one time you should shut the fuck up*

She smiles through the tears and deletes the Snap app. The soldiers are now close enough that she can make out their words. "US military! You are trespassing on federal property. Come out with your hands up."

Her hands shake as she clicks the photo boxes and the trash can icon. She can hear the soldiers' footsteps outside as she slips the phone into her pocket and calls loudly, "For Christ's sake, don't shoot. I'm an American citizen—just a tourist exploring."

————

The soldiers transform the reception area into an informal interview room in which Ambrose sits in an uncomfortable chair. Clad in a large white military tee and camo drawstring shorts that swallow her, she looks small and childish. Being barefoot adds to the illusion. She is aware this is purposeful, a psychological ploy to create a power inequity before an interrogation, and thinks with some irony, *These people have no idea how comfortable I am barefoot and in an oversized tee.*

An armed guard relieved Ambrose of her phone without explanation, while a soldier in a gas mask crammed her clothes in a large red trash bag. A lone soldier flanks Ambrose while others stand sentry just outside the door. Ambrose attempts a casual conversation with the soldier, but he remains as stoic as a palace guard. The dramatics strike her as comical.

The Tall Woman enters with a slightly more friendly greeting and carrying a briefcase. Clearly, she is meant to play the part of the good cop—stern, bound by the rules, but the one who can "help" Ambrose.

"Rather over the top for a tourist simply exploring some old ruins, isn't it?" muses Ambrose.

The Tall Woman smiles. "You have trespassed on marked property of the United States government. That is not taken lightly."

"Right. Trespassing on Park Service property. So why is the military here?"

"The United States government is trustee of this land. She, in her wisdom, may draw upon any resources at her disposal to protect her interest and that of her people."

"Including the interest of the Viequenses?"

"Ambrose, I am not here to engage in political debate. That is far above my pay grade. I am here to inform you that you have trespassed on the property of the United States government, a federal crime that can result in fines and incarceration in a federal facility. Technically, even death if that trespassing is deemed to be treasonous."

"What branch of military so threatens me? Looks like army?"

The Tall Woman fails to reply and opens her briefcase, pulling out a folder with Ambrose's name on it.

Ambrose stares at it, equally horrified and flattered. "Is that a dossier? Do I have a government dossier?"

"Some of your work has shown great patriotism and elevated thought, deeply rooted in democratic ideals that the government values. It's not always a bad thing to have a dossier. We are not the evil conspirators imaginative YouTubers believe us to be."

"But you do take trespassing by a tourist very, very seriously."

"Yes, that we do," acknowledges the Tall Woman as she pulls open the file and a pen from the briefcase and begins making notes.

"No laptop? The government is further behind than taxpayers might hope."

"Wi-Fi on this island can be unreliable."

"Indeed. As can water and electric, and health care."

The Tall Woman doesn't take the bait, moving forward with her interview.

"What was your intent in coming here?"

"To explore."

"How did you know this was here?"

Ambrose shrugs a bit. "It's a small island. Apparently it's rather a lovers' lane among the locals."

"Yes, we do occasionally need to run off young couples."

"Do they get this kind of welcome?"

"Typically, no. They are just local kids looking for some privacy. But a foreign writer with some investigative background raises the interest level."

"I am not a foreigner. This *is* United States soil, as you have pointed out."

"Fair," concedes the Tall Woman.

"And how would you know before you apprehended me that I was a writer with an investigative background?"

"It's a small island, as you have pointed out," the Tall Woman responds with a smile.

"Fair," said Ambrose. The Tall Woman is sharp, and Ambrose likes her.

"What parts of this building have you seen, and why would they be of interest to you?"

"I am ghostwriting a family story. They claimed to have gone to a MEDCOM building, but I couldn't find a record of one."

"Even the military is apt to lose records after half a century."

Ambrose nods assent.

"And what parts of this complex have you explored?"

"Why? What are you hiding?"

Exasperated, the woman responds, "As stated on the signage, on maps, and throughout the island, this compound contains toxic materials. It is our responsibility to monitor exposure to those health hazards."

Ambrose nods. She is almost certain the Tall Woman already knows exactly where she has been, though she doesn't know how. Ambrose wonders if there are trip cameras on-site.

"I entered the hangars and went around to the sheds in the back."

"Did you touch anything?"

"No, not even the door. It was hanging in such a way I could just duck to enter."

"And the sheds. Did you touch them?"

"No."

"Where else did you go on the compound?"

"I came here, opened this door," she says, pointing to the door to the Tall Woman's back, "and entered here. Then opened that door down to the two exam rooms. That's where you found me." She took a chance and left out the lab. For all the Tall Woman's claimed concern for her safety, the questions have centered on what she saw.

"And that's all?"

"Yes."

"Did you come through this door?" She gestures to the northern-facing door.

"No," Ambrose answers, this time honestly.

The Tall Woman shakes her head, puts down her pen, and settles back into her chair, crossing her arms. "Ms. Nobel, this compound contains a multitude of materials that pose serious health hazards. Just behind this building is a fifty-foot pile of asbestos. Inside some of these labs are chemicals that have half-lives of thousands of years. There's a *reason* this area is designated a red zone, and it is nothing more nefarious than trying to protect people from the toxins remaining from industrial usage. You won't find errant tuberculosis virus here and no cover-up by military doctors."

Ambrose goes cold. The Tall Woman knowing who she is and why she is on the island gives her pause. The idea that this military officer could know about her unpublished theories stops her dead. Has the government been spying on her? Monitoring her communications and tracing her contacts?

"How did you know that?"

"It is of no matter. Ms. Nobel, when you choose to explore here, you are choosing to expose yourself to health hazards. And that is one thing. But your being here means I need to deploy my men and expose *them* to health hazards. This incident of yours will cost time, resources, and energy. We will have much work to do when we get back to base."

"What base?" Ambrose inquires.

The Tall Woman grows stern. "You are costing the US government time and money and putting the health of American soldiers—my men— at risk for your folly—chasing false theories. Let me tell you what will happen next. You will be escorted off this compound and back to your hotel. Your plane reservations have been changed. You will take the first flight off the island tomorrow morning. And you will write your book without mention of this place. It is not pertinent to the family story you have been paid to craft. I am leaving you with contact information within the United States government for official input where needed. And you will be very, very grateful that this incident has no further consequences."

The Tall Woman hands Ambrose her phone, which smells of disinfectant. Ambrose takes a moment to let that sink in. She has been kicked out of several churches in her past, a feat of which she was rather proud. But she has never been literally kicked off an island—the manifestation of the modern adage.

"Do I get my clothes back?"

"No," says the Tall Woman pointedly.

Ambrose mumbles, "Well, fuck, that was my favorite sports bra."

She catches the Tall Woman trying, and failing, to hide a sympathetic smile.

CHAPTER 21

A fresh transport picks her up at the edge of Gate G and drops her off at her hotel, the officer in charge leaving her with a stern warning: "Don't leave your room until morning. Food will be brought to you."

"How about a drink?" she asks. The soldier doesn't respond.

Another soldier has driven her golf cart to the guesthouse and parks it out front. A third unmarked car appears and finds beachfront parking facing the hotel. On an island this small, an unmarked car is very obvious. Her minders are making absolute certain she leaves in the morning.

The plucked Trump and a small, dark man Ambrose assumes is her husband are among the late-afternoon diners who witness her eviction from the transport. The Trumpkin proclaims loudly to her husband that this was the libtard she was telling him about. "Certainly glad the military's taking care of the socialist anti-American dumbass," she loudly proclaims from her seat at the bar. Preening her triumph, the woman stares as Ambrose makes her way up the stairs. Ambrose hasn't the time or energy to give her more than an eye roll.

Ambrose enters the fresh Caribbean room and flops on the bed, adrenaline drained. She consciously tries to breathe into rest, knowing a rested mind is important if she's to think clearly, but her mind continues to puzzle over the lab, the military's presence, the history of the island . . . and the visions. Resetting her internet connection to private, she downloads the Snap app and retrieves her messages from Kev and Marcus.

KickboxAmbrose: *OK, formal intros. Kev, this is Marcus, my BJJ trainer and war history guru. Marcus, this is Kev, my cousin and a doctor.*

GermDocK: *Have you seen her apartment?*

2nddegreeMarcus: *Have you seen her gym bag?*

Ambrose smiles, thinking these two will make fast friends, and brings them up to date. Kev is frantic with worry, Marcus full of advice.

She draws sketches of what she couldn't capture in her digital camera— the pile of asbestos, the corn and the farm mixers, the large vats of gas pipes making neat rows into the other building—and Snaps them. She gives a brief overview of the interrogation she underwent at the hands of the Tall Woman, focusing on the gas masks and the reputed health hazards, which concentrate on the northern wing of the lab, the one she didn't enter.

KickboxAmbrose: *Details later. Now: look at the pictures and this sketch. What can you tell me? Marcus, what branch of the military is that? What kind of plane is it?*

KickboxAmbrose: *Kev, anything out of the ordinary for a 1940s exam room or lab? And why the fuck would there be reptiles in the lab?*

GermDocK: *Easy. Pregnancy tests.*

KickboxAmbrose: *???*

GermDocK: *That's how they used to do it. Inject urine taken from the patient into frogs and see if they produced spots. It was time consuming and expensive, though. Only rich women or a woman with a health risk would have been given them*

KickboxAmbrose: *A. The frog thing is so weird. B. Why would the military put that kind of expense into mass pregnancy testing of local women they showed so little concern for?*

There was silence as they absorbed the implications that were unclear but increasingly ominous.

KickboxAmbrose: *Keep researching. I only have till morning*

She lies down again. Knowing the problem is being worked on by her little trusted tribe, and feeling comforted to think of Marcus as trusted, gives her leave for a shallow slumber.

CHAPTER 22

She is awakened by a soft knock at the door. She answers it cautiously to find Lucinda with a tray piled with a triple serving of mahi-mahi tacos, loaded plantains, an Islander, and a shot of *pitorro*. She tears in earnest relief and gratitude. She is ravenously hungry both for food and gracious island hospitality.

"*Mami*, you have made enemies with the military," Lucinda says conspiratorially. She is impressed and proud as she hands over the tray.

Ambrose smiles in spite of herself and the ridiculous situation in which she has found herself. "Apparently I will be checking out early. It has been suggested I take the first flight out tomorrow morning."

"*Sí*, we know," says Lucinda, and Ambrose understands the "we" means the entire island is aware that some kind of incident has taken place with the American who can't drive a golf cart. She then lowers her voice. "Under the plate. *Fuera la Marina! Boricua!*" And quickly she is gone.

Ambrose closes the door firmly before lifting the plate, finding a folded note with scrawled writing: "Another golf cart is parked at the triangle if you need it. I hope you do. *¡Boricua!*"

Ambrose pauses momentarily, wondering how she would start another golf cart, before remembering the keys for the golf carts themselves are all the same. She can drive any golf cart on the island as long as the bike chain from the seat to the steering wheel is unlocked. And she is certain Lucinda has made sure it is. She smiles, shovels the food into her mouth without silverware, and thanks the gods and goddesses Viequenses are very good at quiet disobedience.

The drinks cool her and allow her to rest for another three quarters of an hour. The fish and fruits of the island nourish her body, and she awakes rejuvenated to the sounds of Snaps in the group chat.

2nddegreeMarcus: *plane is a crop spreader—see the pipes under it.*

KickboxAmbrose: *crop spreader? Does that explain the corn silos? Were they really just growing food?*

2nddegreeMarcus: *or altering food*

KickboxAmbrose: *Now there is a thought. Kev, would altering food cause TB like symptoms*

GermDocK: *I don't think so. This was localized to the lungs, it didn't metastasize from the stomach or elsewhere. Whatever it was would need to have been inhaled*

2nddegreeMarcus: *wanna know what the emblem is?*

KickboxAmbrose: 😌 *ummm . . . yes*

2nddegreeMarcus: *took me a while to find. its army. Chemical Warfare Service. Sending you link*

KickboxAmbrose: *We had a chemical warfare service?*

2nddegreeMarcus: *still do*

KickboxAmbrose: *Why would a chemical warfare unit of the army be spreading fertilizer?*

2nddegreeMarcus: *spreading chemicals, of course*

The conversation pauses while they collectively think it through.

KickboxAmbrose: *could they spread asbestos? Seems like it would be too light to really spread.*

2nddegreeMarcus: *mixed with fertilizer to give it weight?*

KickboxAmbrose: *Kev, would that cause mutant TB?*

GermDocK: *I can't know. But, even if you spread asbestos like that, it would still take decades for the disease to develop. These women are still too young*

KickboxAmbrose: *So we aren't really looking for a TB variant. Maybe we are looking for a mesothelioma variant?*

GermDocK: *Maybe. Exposure to some kind of altered asbestos would be closer to the spread pattern than a virus like TB*

2nddegreeMarcus: *and we still don't know why*

Silence for a few moments.

GermDocK: *given their interest in pregnancy tests, what about birth control experiments*

KickboxAmbrose: *The navy had formalized plans to mass evict the natives from the island. Same objective. Different method of getting there?*

2nddegreeMarcus: *that's fucked up*

KickboxAmbrose: *What if it worked? There was a huge drop in population in the 50s and 60s. Infertility experiments in the late 40s would have that effect.*

KickboxAmbrose: *Maybe that's why Philomena never had children.*

2nddegreeMarcus: *Who's Philomena*

KickboxAmbrose: *Not important right now*

GermDocK: *Some kind of altered asbestos might theoretically cause the lung disorders that killed those women. But doesn't make sense that it would cause infertility*

2nddegreeMarcus: *Guess it depends on what they were altering it with. Any ideas, Ambrose?*

KickboxAmbrose: *Other than corn, no. Maybe the other lab—the side I didn't get to—might have some clues?*

GermDocK: *Guess we will never know since you are basically under arrest.*

KickboxAmbrose: *not under arrest. Was just told to be on the plane tomorrow morning. That I will be.*

Kev sends his own eye-roll emoji, followed by *be careful, cuz*

2nddegreeMarcus: *Yeah, even I am thinking you might want to stay put*

She glances out the French doors to judge when the bright Caribbean sun might break to shadows and, with refreshed curiosity, decides to make

good use of her time. As she follows the link to Chemical Warfare Services, she recalls her conversation with Kev regarding medieval warfare—
plague-ridden bodies catapulted into seized cities, effectively turning the
solid defensive stronghold of a walled fortress into a disease zone.

CHEMICAL WARFARE SERVICES

*During the Civil War, Union officials considered using chlorine or hydro-
gen chloride shells to clear Confederates from their battlefield trenches.
The tactic was dismissed as inhumane, especially among brothers, and
since that time the United States has wobbled on its stance of chemical and
biological warfare among a trifecta of humanitarian concerns, defensive
realities, and offensive development. It wasn't until the nature of war
burned global the United States seriously explored chemical weapons.*

*American military forces were woefully unprepared for the poison
battlefields that clouded World War I. In 1915, Germany used chlorine
gas during the battle at Ypres, Belgium, setting the stage for the use of
chemical weapons by both sides for the remainder of the war.*

*The United States bulked for World War I with men and tanks and
firearms but had largely ignored the emerging chemical threat. On the
eve of its entry into the European theater, the United States frantically
assembled a combined forces team led by the army's Medical Department, who hired civilian Dr. Ira Caldwell to lead the effort.*

*A cross-sector team of chemists from government, academia, and indus-
try, especially mining, due to their experience with gas masks, joined
together in converted college laboratories to study chemical warfare,
investigate mass production of chemicals, and develop protective gear and
other solutions. Within the year, more than one thousand scientists and
technicians were dedicated to the effort. The United States itself resisted
the use of chemical weapons during World War I, lacking supplies,
delivery systems, defense, and experience with the weapons, and fearful
of relation by Central Powers with far greater capabilities.*

The fear was not unfounded. One-third of American casualties, over seventy thousand soldiers, were victims of chemical attacks during World War I. It was a slow, painful, inhumane death.

From this hasty beginning, the Chemical Warfare Service (CWS) was formalized by Congress in 1918, with a blue and gold insignia of two chemical reactors crossed over a benzene ring. In 1934, Congress approved the green dragon emblem, the motto "Let Us Rule the Battle by Means of the Elements," and an official CWS song. Inexplicably considering the continued and successful use of chemical weapons by its enemies, Congress defunded much of CWS.

This failure carried over into World War II, where once again Allies faced enemies who possessed far superior chemical and now biological weapon capacity. President Roosevelt announced a retaliation-in-kind policy, an empty threat given the United States had no chemical weapons stockpiles or even the capability to produce biological weapons.

The United States again scrambled to catch up, making rapid investments in CWS and shifting its mission to erect chemical ammunition plants, testing grounds, and defensive equipment. Every US soldier was to be deployed with a gas mask, impregnable suits, and information cards on gas poisoning. More than four hundred chemical battalions and companies with over sixty thousand personnel were created under CWS.

Following World War II, the name of CWS was changed to the Chemical Corps. Roosevelt strongly opposed the change:

"I have a far more important objection to this change of name. It has been and is the policy of this Government to do everything in its power to outlaw the use of chemicals in warfare. Such use is inhumane and contrary to what modern civilization should stand for.

"I am doing everything in my power to discourage the use of gases and other chemicals in any war between nations. While, unfortunately, the defensive necessities of the United States call for study of the use of chemicals in warfare, I do not want the Government of the United States to do anything to aggrandize or make permanent any special bureau of the Army or the Navy engaged in these studies. I hope the time will come when the Chemical Warfare Service can be entirely abolished."

To dignify this Service by calling it the 'Chemical Corps' is, in my judgment, contrary to a sound public policy."

Ambrose breaks with Roosevelt's wisdom to slurp the Islander. She opens the French door to peek for the very obvious unmarked car and confirms its continued surveillance. "Is it sound public policy to spend taxpayer money making sure I get off this little island?" she muses aloud before returning to the tale of the United States' Chemical Corps.

Entering into a new era in the world political theater, the existence of the Chemical Corps was in jeopardy. The War Department, focused now on developing atomic weapons, recommended dissolving the corps. Ironically, what might have saved the Chemical Corps was intel released just prior to a congressional vote reporting Germany had weaponized nerve agents. Congress not only voted to retain the corps but designated it as an official branch of the US Army.

The Korean War, and fear of encountering Russian weapons there, spurred further investments—new training and testing centers and new studies around incendiary munitions, incapacitants, riot control agents, and herbicides. Every branch of the military wanted chemical and biological warfare options for their delivery systems.

The Cold War and its weapons race saw massive investments in chemical and biological weapons, delivery systems, and defensive measures.

The US military's use of napalm in Vietnam prompted public outcry, while domestically there was deepening concern about the effects on communities housing laboratories and testing facilities. A farm near Dugway Proving Ground reported four thousand sheep dying from exposure to poison gas, prompting local protests.

Heavy ground warfare in Iraq during the 1980s and 1990s spurred new concerns of protecting the US military against Soviet-supplied nation-states and terrorist groups with biological and chemical weapons, weapons they had used against their own people.

Today, the continued threat of small nation-states and terrorist groups leads the Chemical Corps to continue its work to defend US military personnel during battles abroad and to defend against international or domestic unexpected high-consequence attacks within her borders. The mission of today's Chemical Corps has been expanded to defend against chemical, biological, radiological, and nuclear hazards as well as other unconventional threats.

The most compelling reason for the continued existence of the Chemical Corps? History shows that those countries and peoples without such weapons capability are those most at risk of being attacked.

A buzzing from her phone pulls her from her laptop.

RickCortez: *Aunt P nearing the end. She asked for you.*

KickboxAmbrose: *I'm on Vieques. Coming back tomorrow. Will come from airport. Tell her to hang on.*

And then a group Snap:

GermDocK: *Well, we found your Dr. Ira Caldwell—a founder of CWS*

2nddegreeMarcus: *yep*

KickboxAmbrose: *I'm going back up. Stay by your phones. I'll send photos as I take them—JIC*

Glancing out the French doors, she checks to see that the black unmarked car is still stationed out front. She sprays with bug spray and Florida water, grabs her glasses and the golf cart key, and scampers through the back door and down the small fire escape. She circumvents the road, trying to casually slip through the backyards of half-abandoned hotels and eateries, until she reaches the only traffic triangle on the island. There, just as Lucinda has promised, is a golf cart with the lock device hanging useless.

She escapes, driving to Gate G. Afraid that someone might be following her, she hides the golf cart as best she can in low, prickly foliage before following the horse shit trail, which becomes more difficult with dusk curtaining the island.

The hike gives her time to process the events from the past twenty-four hours. Fertilizer spreaders, asbestos, a secret medical center. Logical connections between them lie just beyond her reach. Maybe there is no connection at all. But the pregnancy tests, the denial of the medical center's existence—there must have been some kind of mass fertility experiments. And God knows what else. It is fact the military tried to rid itself of the natives for decades. Instead of risking a public outcry from relocating, maybe they planned to eradicate the population by means of secret mass coerced sterilization?

And *that* is why Philomena had no children. Not because God or Santa Marta was angry with her. Not because she owed a debt for a life taken. Philomena needed to know.

Snap chirps.

2nddegreeMarcus: *googled corn 1940s chemical warfare. wanna know what I got?*

KickboxAmbrose: *i do*

He sends a picture of his screen displaying a chemical formula: an O to the left, two lines leading into a split with CH_3 on either side. Acetone (C_3H_6O).

KickboxAmbrose: *Acetone? Like nail polish remover?*

2nddegreeMarcus: *yep. back then it was made in the lab with massive amounts of* 🌽

GermDocK: *and it causes infertility*

KickboxAmbrose: *nail polish remover causes infertility?*

GermDocK: *In high enough doses or for long enough times of exposure— yes even today nail technicians are at risk*

2nddegreeMarcus: *So they create some kind of hybrid between acetone and asbestos, mixed with fertilizer and disbursed by airplane. Is it possible, Kev?*

GermDocK: *no idea. am not a chemist. but if it were possible, it would be disastrous.*

KickboxAmbrose: *i'm just at the site again i'll send pics.*

She passes by the hangar with the fertilizer plane and heads straight for the false MEDCOM building. When she ducks into the receptionist area, she opens the door to her left and follows a steep flight of stairs into a cavernous warehouse with walls lined in a black rubbery substance and towering ancient equipment.

It is impossibly spacious, and she realizes the structures must be half underground. It is humid, with the dank smell of rubber and decaying insects, with high notes of nail polish remover. Acetone. Half industrial, half laboratory, rows of large, peeling vats with pipes and wheel valves and gauges line the right wall. Smaller mixers that mirror the portable agricultural mixers outdoors lie in neat rows next to the vats.

The left wall is lined with lab stations—counters, white medical cabinets, flasks, and Bunsen burners, a few tall stools still waiting for technicians. She opens Snap, but she has lost the signal in the lined subterranean lab. She walks slowly, finding her bearings as she travels, guided by camera light. The light doesn't penetrate far enough into the dark to capture the scale of the place—she senses more than sees its enormity.

The lab countertops lie underneath white, peeling medical cabinets with thick glass bottles, metal tongs, and platforms with glass flasks, small, disintegrating hoses still attached at their bases. Each station boasts an identical series of plaques—a few hazard warnings and safety signs and two chemical formulas. The first formula is overly complicated. The second she recognizes from Marcus's picture. Acetone.

She comes to the end of the long row of stations. Here at the back of the building are vats of a different kind, painted bright red and covered with large, shriveling warning stickers. These vats are labeled "napalm," "mustard gas," "carbonyl chloride."

For the first time, she realizes she may be in danger from something other than the military. She commits to making this a very quick trip. Her light follows pipes poking from the tops of the hazardous vats toward the ceiling and angling toward the left. They lead into another doorway, past a small office with a desk and clipboard, to several chambers. She enters one.

The chamber door is at least a foot thick, with a small observational window and a sliding door at the bottom, like a cell at a mental institution. The pipes end in the chamber ceiling, feeding into smaller pipes and mechanical vents. The chamber is lined with that same black rubbery substance, save for a small, barred window akin to the one she climbed yesterday in the exam room and an obvious two-way mirror. The black lining has been carved, presumably by the cell's inhabitants. Horror sickens her as realization sets in. She runs her finger over the etchings. Some are tallies made in an effort to grasp at reality by marking cycles of the sun; others are drawings; some are hearts with initials; others humorous or obscene. Names etched could still be read. One is fainter than the others. She reaches out and caresses the faint "J" with her finger and this time almost anticipates the blurred vision that clears and the strong smell of roasting coffee and honey.

A teenage boy jumps from the military transport, one of a dozen such boys following orders barked from a barrel-chested sergeant. "Gentlemen, you are now the property of the United States Army. Disembark and line up at attention. Do you know what attention is?"

This boy is more frail than the others, with thick brown hair top-heavy on his small frame. He helps another boy who is struggling to make the jump with his duffel bag, and the sergeant screams, "Private, do you believe the private is incapable of carrying a duffel bag?"

The boys start, unaccustomed to screaming and confused by the question. The sergeant turns to the struggling private, and the boy notices an ugly red blotched birthmark on the back of his neck, seeping into his hairline.

"Private, this private believes you are unable to carry your own duffel bag. I assure you, Private, that the United States Army has every confidence that you are able to carry your own duffel bag. Are you capable of carrying your own duffel bag, Private?"

"Yes, sir," the boy stumbles.

"That is correct. The private is *capable of carrying his own duffel bag."*

The sergeant turns his ire to the boy with top-heavy hair. "What is your name, Private?"

"Javier, sir. Javier Cortez."

"Cortez? You come from that huge family, with all those damn kids?"

"Sí."

"Don't you fucking 'sí' me. You are now the property of the United

States Army, Private Cortez. You will speak English and only English. I and every member of the United States Army speak English. If I or any other member of the United States Army hears any other language spoken, we logically assume an enemy is in our midst and will take action appropriate to assure the elimination and destruction of that enemy. Do you understand, Private Cortez?"

"Yes, sir," Sweet Javier manages.

"Now, Private Cortez, do you come from that huge family, with all those damn kids?"

"Yes, sir," Private Cortez repeats.

"Jesus H. Christ, boy. Your people must love to fuck. Your mama must love to fuck. Your daddy must love to fuck. Hell, I bet those sisters of yours love to fuck. Do you love to fuck, Private Cortez?"

"I ... I don't know, sir." Sniggering ripples through the group, and Sweet Javier reddens.

"No, I wouldn't assume you would, Private Cortez. You look like you might faint dead if your dick got hard.

"Your brother came home in a casket, didn't he, Private Cortez?" the sergeant continues.

"Yes, sir." Private Cortez's voice strengthens.

"Then what the fuck are you doing here, Private Cortez? Do you want to come home in a casket, too, Private Cortez?"

"I want to honor my brother, sir."

The sergeant steps closer to Javier, eyes narrowed, his breath reeking of tobacco chaw, twin scars on his cheek reddening. The sergeant stands, hawking over Javier for a long, purposefully painful draw. "You want revenge, don't you? You believe the United States Army owes you revenge, Private Cortez, for the honor it gave your brother to give his life in her glorious service?"

Javier doesn't answer—he doesn't know how. Every answer here is the wrong answer. The sergeant leans in as he whispers, "If you ever see your sisters again, you tell them I said hi." Then he backs away, straightens, and addresses Sweet Javier more officially.

"Private Cortez, in the graciousness of the United States Army I am going to give you some revenge. Step to the side, Private Cortez. The United States Army has a special assignment for you."

———

He lies on the ground, his head resting on a military-issued tee that was once stark white. Now it is filthy, as is he. His frail frame is sunken, his hair matted with unnatural bald spots, his skin patched with burns and blisters.

The room is large and empty, with lined blackened walls and a heavy sealed door. The southern side of the room has a small, high window with iron bars slating thick glass. The northern side shines dark reflections, obviously a two-way mirror to anyone familiar enough with the concept. Sweet Javier is not familiar enough.

The measured roaring of an approaching military transport rouses him. He listens as the transport stops close by, and a tide of muffled voices washes over him, careless and laughing. He jumps several times before he catches the bars on the high window and struggles to pull himself up and hang, allowing a narrow view of the tarmac. He recognizes most as they disembark from the transport—his neighbors and extended family. They greet soldiers with friendly waves, gratefully accepting bars of chocolate and bags of bread as he has done countless times, and enter MEDCOM.

He sees his sisters—Rosie and Philomena. Screaming and desperate, he pounds with one fist on the thick glass, his other hand slowly sliding down the rusted bars. His feet flail, pushing against the wall, desperate to find leverage. Panicked, he slowly loses his grasp. As he collapses under his own frail weight, panic leaves him, ceding to sickening acceptance. Something in his eyes changes, just as the ceiling vents click open.

He knows what comes after that click, and this time he stands to greet it, inhaling the toxic fog deeper instead of lying low and choking it away. He jumps and grabs the bars again, this time positioning himself toward the vents rather than the window. Gratefully he gulps the vent's poison in huge, desperate swallows, suckling till they run dry, hungry to finally die.

He crumbles to the floor when the fog stops. When the figures enter wearing white lab coats and gas masks, he doesn't fight them. He lets them shine the bright light in his fading eyes and prick his arm. He watches emotionlessly as he bleeds into a neat vial marked "Hispanic male, 17" and hears alarm in their American voices as they read the wrapped cuff on his arm. He smiles a bit as he lifts triumphantly toward a reward he will gladly share with his beloved brother.

Her fingers jolt back from the etching; she is breathing heavily, tears stinging her raw cheeks. The childish inscription from the cemetery—"Come Home"—hits differently now. Sweet Javier never left.

The rumblings of military transports focus her attention back to the present. Guessing she has forty-five seconds, she returns to the small office and rifles through drawers and filing cabinets. Unlike the desk at the main reception area, these have not been cleared out. She flips through aged, sepia folders and yellowed paper with typewriter fonts. It smells like the historic section of the library—musty and mysterious. Words jump out as she flips through neatly organized charts with hand-written notes—napalm, mustard gas, carbonyl chloride—along with dosages, vital signs, and horrifying observation notes: "ulcerations," "blisters," "blindness," "coughing," and, coldly, "expiration."

There are no names, only case numbers divided by ethnicity: Puerto Rican, Mexican, Hispanic, Negro, with data rows labeled "Control Data: Caucasian."

Holy shit. They were testing reactions to chemical weapons between races. On their own people. On their own soldiers. She is so astounded she jumps at the expected intrusion of a swarm of armed, gas-masked guards. She puts her hands up and allows them to apprehend her, pat her down, and take her phone. Knowing there is no way out, she is docile as the uniformed men surround her, escort her roughly to the darkened tarmac.

She is led toward a transport parked close to the false MEDCOM building. The Tall Woman stands erect in her perfect pencil skirt near a second transport, chatting with a civilian in wrinkled suit pants, hands sheepishly poised in pockets, and Ambrose senses the familiarity and momentarily doubts it. Why would he be in Vieques? She stops in her tracks, processing the betrayal, while the soldiers on each side tug forward at the resistance.

And then it happens, in motion so slow that his expression will be permanently cast on her memory, and so quickly she can't recall how, moments later, she came to be in the back of the transport, handcuffed and surrounded by soldiers.

Will is clearly surprised. He did not expect to be seen by her. And when she sees him, she triggers. She easily breaks free from the careless grasp of the soldiers and charges him. His deer-in-the-headlights expression gives way to lifting eyebrows, shaking of his head, and desperation in his eyes. "Ambrose, it's not what you think." Soldiers descend upon her. She dispenses of the first with a grappled head pulled into a bulleted knee. The second, approaching from behind, is rewarded with a brutal elbow to the face, followed by a crippling kick to the kidney. The third approaches straight on. She waits until he is close, times an angled shot into a one-kneed fireman's carry that flips him over her shoulder and lands him on the ground. Landing crouched, she follows with a quick elbow, enough to ensure he stays down. Even through her rage, as she launches toward her target, she recognizes she has finally executed the fireman's carry—breathing into it, using the soldier's momentum against him, and with fluid timing. Marcus would have been proud.

Still Will stands, backed against the transport, eyes wide, before cowering into a crouched, half-standing fetal position. She knows he is defenseless. She doesn't care. She hates him more for it. She sets strong and steady, swats his cowering forearms down with a batted jab to expose his crooked nose as her power hand curls to her chin and twists back to launch just as she is clawed back from behind. Raging, she pushes against her apprehenders, using her momentum to throw a high push kick that would have decimated him had it not been shortened by tugging from behind.

Even as she is swarmed and dragged, his narcissistic delusions of saviorhood self-justify the depths of his betrayal. His desperate voice reaches her: "Ambrose, I am trying to protect you."

CHAPTER 23

She sits on a purposefully uncomfortable metal chair in a gray cinderblock room with overhung lights and an imposing table. "Rather cliquish, isn't it?" she greets the Tall Woman as she enters the room.

"Rather," smiles the Tall Woman, tucking her perfectly ironed pencil skirt under her properly. They sit for a long moment facing each other, teetering a bit on a trifecta of friendship, foe, and mutual respect. Ambrose considers that the Tall Woman would make a fine sparring partner.

The Tall Woman motions to the oversize military tee and sweats Ambrose now wears. "Starting a collection?"

Ambrose smiles, and they fall silent.

A master negotiator, the Tall Woman waits in neutrality for Ambrose to begin.

"How cheap did he sell me? Let me guess—fifteen minutes of fame?"

"He was sure he could persuade you to drop the story in Philly, that he had a certain power over you. He was deeply embarrassed, and I was rather amused, when you proved him wrong."

"His ego knows no bounds."

The Tall Woman laughs. "His ego makes him insufferable but also makes him very easy to navigate."

"You and I might could be friends," quips Ambrose.

"For what it's worth, he earnestly believed he was protecting you—saving you from exactly this. Your martyred white knight who you cruelly misunderstand. His affection for you is real, at least as real as he is capable of."

"I will give him that he is always the first to drink his own snake oil. I always thought he was one of those people who could pass a lie detector with flying colors, he so believed his own lies."

"Yes, I suspect he could," concedes the Tall Woman.

"Will you give him his fifteen minutes?"

"Not in the way he thinks."

The women share a knowing smile, and Ambrose trusts the Tall Woman will offer Will a just and karmic reward.

"Being our guest, having connections, makes him feel important, feeds his ego. And for that he gave us his full cooperation. You, though, Ambrose, will not sell yourself so cheaply." The Tall Woman leans in. "Ambrose, we are on the same side here. You cannot tell this story. Why would you want to? What could possibly be achieved?"

"Truth. Justice. Jesus Christ, you killed your own people—used them as guinea pigs. It was no better than Hitler, while you were fighting Hitler! Javier Cortez. You promised that boy glory and revenge and then killed him—tortured him. He died here, under your watch—your own soldier."

"The military has long admitted that mistakes were made."

"Not these mistakes. The military has not admitted to or taken responsibility for *these* mistakes. The government doesn't admit to testing airborne birth control on natives. Did you know that Philomena believes it's her fault—that she angered God and he punished her by making her barren? She deserves to be sent to her God in peace, not in fear," Ambrose continues, putting together the pieces as she talks.

"And they certainly don't know those boys died here, right in their home, without ever leaving the island. His family doesn't even have a body to bury. That's just one family. How many were there? The trauma that has been done on this island, our people . . . "

"These people are not going to be helped by this revelation, Ambrose. Admitting fault and being responsible are two different things. The truth is we are often put in position of quietly taking moral responsibility without politically admitting mistakes . . . It was a different time," the Tall Woman explains. "We cannot judge yesterday's action with today's morals. I promise you, now we *are* trying to make amends how we can, with what we have. What will help these people—"

"*Our* people," Ambrose interjects, and the Tall Woman concedes.

"*Our* people. What will help our people now is tourism, jobs, access to health care and food, all of which are being addressed through US-funded initiatives built on very delicate renewed relationships. If this story gets out, you undermine that work, you diminish that renewed trust, and you jeopardize our sincere efforts to make things right—for this whole population, Ambrose, not just for one family who was lucky enough to escape. We *are* trying to fix this for these people."

"*Our* people. And they aren't broken," Ambrose asserts. "You are a true believer, all passion and righteousness for your cause. You believe the United States is the most powerful force in the world. And the most righteous." Ambrose pauses long enough for the Tall Woman to shrug an agreement.

"The US military—the strongest military force in the world—tried in every conceivable way to destroy them. You stole their land, their jobs, their farms. You destroyed the entire economy and purposefully blocked new investors. You raped their women and forced their sons to war. You tried to unilaterally evict them—twice. You used both the land and the people as lab rats—tests so vile you wouldn't perform them on your enemies. You bombed the island for sixty years straight. Sixty years! You dumped toxic waste with a half-life of millions of years on its soil—over and over and over again. And just recently, after two back-to-back hurricanes, the US allowed its own citizens to go without electric and water for over a year—that would never happen on the mainland. And the government has lied and denied and dodged responsibility for all of it, intervening only where military interests are served."

Ambrose continues, "And yet this tiny defenseless population—with no weapons, no military, no political voice, no money, no one even knowing or caring they exist—has survived. Not just survived but thrived with dignity and honor and grace. If you were to leave this island right now, they would survive just fine. You need them far more than they need you. Seems to me that kind of resilience—that kind of survivor mindset in the face of sustained aggression—might be of interest to the world's mightiest military. Maybe instead of fixing them, your goals would be better served if you learned from them."

The Tall Woman is silent for the longest of minutes. This time she is the one who breaks the silence, echoing Ambrose's earlier words: "You and I might could be friends."

Emboldened, Ambrose ventures to test a theory she can't yet prove.

"You still make biological and chemical weapons here. Not just what was left behind. And you know damn well what 'unidentified substances' are. It's here. The red zone is a red herring to keep people away." Ambrose takes the Tall Woman's silence as verification that there is at least some truth in her suspicions.

"And you know this island is close to the Puerto Rico Trench—to Milwaukee Deep. What happens to all that shit—biological warfare, chemical weapons, nuclear waste, whatever else you have developed—when a fucking earthquake happens? We are overdue, you know. What happens when whatever safeguards you have fail in an earthquake or a tsunami?"

The Tall Woman's studied, FBI-interrogator facade breaks as she looks away. The scenario is a question with no answer and exactly the scenario that keeps the Tall Woman up at night. The punch has landed where it hurts.

Ambrose's tone softens. "When that happens, you might very well need people like the Viequenses." Her softening is too late. Ambrose admires the quickness with which the Tall Woman regains her composure, switches tactics, and exploits Ambrose's own weakness, counterpunching somewhere it hurts.

"There are other personal considerations . . ." The Tall Woman stiffens and cliffs.

"What other considerations?"

"You have put Marcus and Kevin in a peculiar position."

"How do you know about Marcus and Kevin?"

The Tall Woman doesn't answer. Ambrose's chest tightens, close to panic. "You're tracing my phone. Are you threatening them?"

"No, Ambrose, I am not threatening them." The Tall Woman uses a calming tone that ensures she is indeed threatening them, without politically taking responsibility. "We are also aware you have spent significant resources in pursuit of very American values. We admire your tenacity and wish to broadly support that kind of storytelling."

"You're bribing me?"

"No. I am offering you a positive way out. This is not a fight you can win. But we can split the card well. We have very liberal resources, Ambrose. What would it take?"

Silence.

"I will give you a few moments for consideration. May I bring you some coffee?" says the Tall Woman as she rises, displaying her full height and her still-perfect pencil skirt. Ambrose nods distractedly as the Tall Woman leaves.

One of the greatest lessons learned from fighting is to remember your objective. Fighters who give in to emotion, who fight for ego or seek flashy knockouts, often lose both themselves and the fight because they lose the objective. The objective in the ring is simple—score more points. Giving in to emotion, ego fighting, and seeking flashy knockouts often lead away from that objective.

The lesson works in life as well. Most often, the lesson simplifies and calms decisions. Is your objective to be right or to preserve a relationship?

If your objective is to fix an error the bank made, are you drawn closer to that objective by berating the teller? If your objective is to save up for a Hellcat, is buying fancy coffee every day pulling you toward or away from that objective?

Where life gets complicated is when objectives themselves are in conflict. Is her objective to tell a family story? To expose the wrongs of the military? To help a people by telling their story? To stroke the writer's ego she acknowledges exists within her? To be right in the face of Will? To prevent Marcus from seeing her as a failure? And what actions will pull her toward or away from those objectives? She calculates carefully how close she can get, in her present situation, to meeting any of the expectations and the diminishing returns if she fails to act now.

The Tall Woman is at least partially right—with the limited proof she has right now and the military inclined to block the story, it will be difficult to achieve any kind of exposé or any large-scale change. That may have to wait for another time. But what she can do now is bring peace to one person, comfort to one family. She sighs. For all the work that went in, for the sweat and tears and the passion, it will end in a draw.

The Tall Woman reenters, handing Ambrose a Styrofoam cup with a quizzical yet patient look. She settles into the chair, folding her skirt beneath her.

Ambrose takes a sip of the coffee and winces at the watery, bitter taste. She has grown accustomed to the rich, smooth, nutty brew of the island. She looks into the weak, overly hot brew as if it were soothsayer tea leaves and faces the Tall Woman.

"I need to tell the story once. Just in a whisper. To a dying woman."

The Tall Woman nods.

"So, Ambrose, speak. What else do you want?"

Backed into a corner, panicked, realizing the ones she most cares about are the most threatened, Ambrose pauses, calms, breathes into it, and finds her voice.

CHAPTER 24

She drives straight from the airport across the rolling farmland outside of Philly to Philomena's small cottage. Rick opens the door before she knocks, expecting her. They exchange a look of knowing but have no time for words. He motions a stay to the family gathered in the living room and opens the bedroom door for Ambrose.

Philomena is in her cozy bed with a quilt stitched of mismatched and perfectly harmonious squares. She looks tired and frail, though comfortable. Her santo has been moved to her nightstand, and a young, handsome priest is at her side. Her ancestral aura is heavy and near, and Ambrose mourns not just for her friend but for the world about to lose a treasure it doesn't know it has.

The young priest offers his chair. She bristles reflexively as he moves past her to another chair in a corner of the room out of earshot. Philomena smiles as Ambrose draws close.

"Did you find the message in the graveyard?"

"Yes. But, Philomena, I found so much more. I *saw* so much more."

"*Sí*, those who have been through much can see much. I told you your eyes were not bad. Just meant to see different things. Use that sight well. Remember the message in the graveyard. You will need it for life's next chapter."

"I promise, but right now, I need you to listen carefully." And she spends several minutes whispering in Philomena's ear. She pulls away and ends, "Philomena, that is why you didn't have children. Not because God was mad at you. It was not a divine punishment but man's brutality. Go to your God in peace."

"*Mija*, you came all this way to tell me this?"

"Of course."

"Ambrose, it *was* God's wrath, payment for my sins. The military are only his pawns. There's only one way to go home well. I've never been able to speak it. Help me do it now, Ambrose, and never speak of it to my family. Promise me."

Philomena's gaze wanders toward her santo. Now, having visited Vieques, Ambrose knows the santo is not of a black Virgin Mary with Jesus on her lap. It is Santa Marta la Dominadora with the orphaned child she saved from snakes cuddled on her lap. The dark, wild, sensual Puerto Rican goddess is known to slay dragons, dominate men, and live in the cemetery. If you are brave enough to ask her favor, it is said her preferred offering is rich black coffee and honey.

Ambrose takes a coin from her pocket, one she received on Vieques. She offers it to the east, to the west, to the south, and to the north, then lays it among the tangled snakes at Santa Marta's feet before cradling in her hands the rosary snuggled at her side. The beads' smooth surfaces feel familiar draped over her hand.

Reluctantly, knowing it must be done, she gives a beckoning glance to the youthful priest, who rises quickly, eager to be of service and unaware of Ambrose's inner struggle. He stands respectfully over the entwined duo. Ambrose has a moment of panic as she realizes the priest has unknowingly trapped her in the corner. She panics and fights the dark closet from appearing in her mind, from the Easter purple folding into itself and the smell of turning seafood. This time, calling upon the strength of Santa Marta la Dominadora and Philomena, she dominates her trauma.

Ambrose and Philomena join together in invocation, one voice strengthening as the other wanes, "Bless me, Father, for I have sinned . . . "

The priest softly assures atonement, and somewhere in the hallowed chain of whispered Hail Marys, Philomena Cortez's rosary-draped chest empties of breath and fills with grace.

EPILOGUE

His silhouette deepens with dusk as he stands, balding head reflecting the wanning sun, hands tucked sheepishly in wrinkled suit pockets, watching her from the street for some time. Eventually, reluctantly, he turns and slowly walks away, his head lowered.

Inside the club, she senses something familiar and aching, like an aura before a migraine. Lowering her gloved hands, pulling her headphones to her neck, she turns a searching gaze toward the large picture window fronting Ground Zero. Impressionistic shadows against the crimson sky mirage sight, but a visceral knowing freezes her in her stance as Pat Benatar's "We Belong" escapes her headphones.

———

A foreman in a white hard hat and bright-yellow vest yells directions in Spanish to backhoe drivers while dozens of local workers with blue hard hats and union emblems busily shovel and move large pipes into place. The sprawling cement foundation takes shape under a banner with three flags—the castled flag of Vieques, the one star of Puerto Rico, and the fifty stars of America—proudly announcing, "Future site of the Sweet

Javier General Hospital and the Philomena Cortez Children's Wing."

———

Gathered around a table in a modest kitchen, a large Cortez family of cousins and aunts and siblings finishes the last decade of the rosary in Philomena's honor. In unison, they cross themselves, pass their rosaries to a small, altered table donning both a statue of the Virgin Mary and Philomena's Santa Marta santo, and joyously turn their attention to passing rich coffee and *pitorro* and *pasteles*. A raw, typed manuscript is opened, and highlighted passages are read aloud. The family laughs and cries and argues about how events unfolded and how they didn't. Rick scribbles notes in the margins for Ambrose, translating the elders' Spanish. Occasionally, at the mention of Philomena's name, an aunt pulls a coin from the tin and places it lovingly in a copper bowl at Santa Marta's feet. And for a moment, Santa Marta's lips part to a sensual smile.

———

Back at the fight club, Ambrose grabs her glove bag and car keys. She vaults over mats and shields toward the door, where she pauses. In the mirrored reflection of the window, she catches the sight of tousled curls. True to Pavlov's observation, her heart quickens. She breathes, easing into it, allowing her face to soften into a grin. He may never mature into the solid ground the surface of her life needs. But she concedes this cosmic, elemental truth written in the stars and prismed in the ocean: he dips the surface of her reality; he flutters her navigation. He is her Milwaukee Deep. Her softening is rewarded with that perfectly imperfect fighter's grin. Their gaze holds briefly. The energy of the fight hasn't yet left them.

Bouncing into the parking lot, she twirls the car key ring around her fingers. Her walk slows as she runs her hand across the classic muscular body with a gunmetal-gray finish and dark-tinted windows. She circles to the driver's side, appreciating the "GhostWriterLLC" vanity plate. She settles into the rich leather interior and caresses the wheel with a contented smirk before roaring the engine to life. The dashboard awakens with a red "Challenger Hellcat" icon and Pat Benatar's "We Belong" switches from her headsets to the speakers. *We belong to the light, we belong to the thunder . . .* She shifts down, owning her power.

We belong, we belong together.

————

It has taken more than five decades of work, tens of thousands of failures, each failure succeeding in making tiny, incremental progress, weakening with every attempt the aging tarmac. Until one day, as Ambrose drives away in her Hellcat a thousand miles away, the impossible happens . . . one delicate bud breaks through the solid layer of crushed rock and tar, just at the apex of the military numeric "9." The triumph of persistence is a glorious feat, no less so for being unobserved by man. This delicate bud—the one-in-a-trillion chosen one—flings open its arms, saluting the Caribbean sun and the salt air that has weakened the tarmac from the top while generations of seeds attack from the bottom, a battle of nature bringing the two together in this one heroic moment. Sunlight bathes the floret in its victory, just as the little emerging bud, entwined deep within the island, and the island entwined deep within the Puerto Rican trench begins to tremble and quake . . .

ACKNOWLEDGMENTS

I traveled to Vieques the first week the island opened following the pandemic. Against the backdrop of that global tragedy, the kinship and resilience of the island community shone a bit brighter, hit a bit different. I met many along the way—golf cart renters, waiters, innkeepers, families picnicking on the beach, ranchers chasing naughty horses—and all welcomed me as family. I remain deeply touched and changed by the island's embrace. Assumptions I made about the community's attitudes toward the military's presence were fundamentally challenged, and *Milwaukee Deep* reflects a much more layered and textured story due to the input of those who truly own that story. I believe Viequenses hold an enormous reserve of untapped wisdom about creating predator-proof communities and healthful responses to trauma, and I aspire to have this work lead to further exploration.

I hope my work serves the island, its people, survivors of trauma, and the mixed martial arts community with integrity. I remain open to corrections, suggestions, and alternate viewpoints. It is my intention that this work, in its successes and in its failures, may be used to forward understanding. Where the story fails, I take sole responsibility.

Where the story succeeds, I owe those who have guided my work and influenced my life.

Editors are a first and last line of defense. They don't prevent you from being stupid, but they do prevent your stupidity from being globally exposed. Marie Lanser Beck patiently and lovingly shaped this story. This work, and all of my writing, has been uplifted by the gracious sharing of her rare intuitive crafting of story. Jessica McClearly's sharp eyes and bold red lines, coupled with earnest encouragement, steadied my trembling voice. If I am the mother of this work, surely Marie and Jessica are the midwives.

One of the reasons I chose Mascot Books to publish this work was Jess Cohn, the creator of Mascot's imprint Subplot. She exuded such belief and ownership in Subplot, I felt I found someone as personally invested in the success of this project as me. I am grateful for her passion, professionalism, and patience and look forward to seeing Subplot rise under her studied care.

My launch team gave me advice throughout the unfamiliar territory of publishing and marketing and the endless decisions that are a part of that process. I sometimes wavered in my own decision-making, but I never questioned their collective wisdom. Thank you to Heather McEndree, Diane Chamberlain, and Michelle D'Antonio, and other members of my launch team acknowledged elsewhere.

Keeping a business running, plus opening Mission Solved Inc, while also writing a book would simply not be possible without my co-creators at Ghost Writer, who held our mission steadfast while I researched and traveled and wrote about the story of Vieques: Colleen Tidd, Christina Williams, Jack Hubbard, Theresa DiLoreta, Meg Partington, Mira Sullivan, Judy Chambers, and Steph Mummert.

Thanks to Tanner Matthews and Gracie Waller for their valued input into Brazilian jiu jitsu and Puerto Rico, respectively. This story owes to you fireman's carry take-downs and *pitorro*!

Enormous gratitude to the mixed martial arts community who embrace an "everyone an athlete" philosophy. Thank you to the welcoming crew at Elite Martial Arts in Pennsylvania; the straight-up badass tribe at Bowerhouse in Frederick, Maryland (bowerhouseacademy.com), especially the brains of Chris Bower, the warrior soul of Terry "The Duke" Bartholomew, and the encouraging heart of Steph Caffrey; Claudie Kenion from Capitol Punishment in Harrisburg, Pennsylvania (capitolpunishmentboxing.com), who trains equity of opportunity along with uppercuts; and the five-star WBO Gym (wbofit.com), also in Pennsylvania, where, unbeknownst to them, many a writer's block is overcome while I deadlift or treadmill. I keep a notebook and pen in that little pink boxing bag.

To my lifelong supporters, Amy Viverette Cowan, Karen Kaczmarak Taylor, Susan Madden Grimes, and Theresa Healey Chiotos, who believed me a writer long before I had the courage to call myself such, thank you for loving me through discovery.

To my family, Cris and Jack, who never needed to believe me a writer or an athlete or an entrepreneur, who may never crack this book to read this dedication, because to them I need be nothing but theirs, I am.

ABOUT THE AUTHOR

K irstie Croga is an author, athlete, and entrepreneur. Her life epitomizes the power of the pen to change the world. Her work with nonprofits and NGOs across the globe gives her a unique perspective on social issues and the ability to spin the honest, complex, sometimes raw tale of our human condition into fast-paced, humorous, and intriguing story-telling. Ghost Writer LLC, an award-winning business she founded in 2017, embraces a mission of "Writing a better human story." Ghost Writer employs powerful storytelling to amplify the world-changing missions of nonprofit organizations. Kirstie also founded Mission Solved Inc, a nonprofit supporting emerging adults with childhood trauma, broadband equality, literacy, and "everyone an athlete" programming.

Kirstie enjoys boxing, weightlifting, and running, and adores watching football (favoring her beloved New England Patriots). She is most content writing in her big, comfy chair in front of the fireplace with her overgrown collie at her feet.